continued .

"A moving portrayal of the survival of the human spirit in times of conflict. [The cellist's] gesture ties the different strands of the book, involving three people who come to recognize both the futility of war and the insidious ways in which it threatens our shared humanity. . . . Galloway gives us valuable insights into how compassion can blossom, unexpectedly, during mindless atrocities. *The Cellist of Sarajevo* is an accomplished, important work." —*Chicago Sun-Times*

"A stripped-down depiction of the siege of Sarajevo in the 1990s. . . . Galloway uses admirable restraint—the shelling of a crowded water station becomes all the more horrible. . . compelling." —*Entertainment Weekly*

"Unusual for a book about war, *The Cellist of Sarajevo* manages to convey a sense of hope for humanity. Inspired by the true story of a cellist who daily risked his life to play his music in a street where twenty-two died waiting to buy bread, Steven Galloway's fine novel takes readers inside the horrors of the siege of Sarajevo. Mr. Galloway tells the story of the city's suffering from the viewpoints of three people who have lived there in good times and bad. It's physically a small book with small tensions surrounding a big subject. What touches the reader most is the way individuals slowly and quietly come to see how important it is not to lose their soul. Mr. Galloway points out that in the future, the world may well forget the horrors of Sarajevo." —*The Dallas Morning News*

"I cannot imagine a lovelier, more beautifully wrought book about the depravity of war than *The Cellist of Sarajevo*. Each chapter is a brief glimpse at yet another aspect of the mind, the heart, the soul—altogether Galloway gives us fine, deep notes of human music, which will remain long after the final page."

—ZZ Packer,
author of *Drinking Coffee Elsewhere*

"Steven Galloway's *The Cellist of Sarajevo* is a wonderful story, a tribute to the human spirit in the face of insanity."

—Kevin Baker,
author of *Dreamland* and *Paradise Alley*

"A tense and haunting novel following four people trying to survive war-torn Sarajevo. With wonderfully drawn characters and a stripped-down narrative, Galloway brings to life a distant conflict." —*Publishers Weekly*

"Steven Galloway's street-level view of the siege of Sarajevo . . . isn't sentimental, but it's very beautiful." —*Paste Magazine*

"Four people struggle to stay alive in war-torn Sarajevo, remembering the simple pleasures of their old routines as they settle into horrifying, desperate new ones. Indelible imagery and heartbreaking characters give authority to this chilling story and make human a crisis typically overlooked in literature." —*Kirkus Reviews* (starred review)

continued . . .

"A bread line in besieged Sarajevo. A mortar lobbed by Serb soldiers on the hill. Death for twenty-two people. A cellist sees it all and determines to honor the dead. . . . And so Galloway opens his first novel, inspired by true events, weaving together four lives to tell the awful story of Sarajevo's devastation. Galloway writes simply and affectingly . . . hitting a sweet, clear note that makes the siege of Sarajevo very real."

—*Library Journal*

"The work of an expert, *The Cellist of Sarajevo* is a controlled and subtle piece of craftsmanship."   —*The Guardian*

"Captivating . . . ambitious and exquisitely wrought. . . . Sensuous and precise, Galloway's prose captures the unbidden movement between personal and public space, the contradiction of being trapped in a city one would not think of leaving, even if one could."   —*Globe and Mail*

"Steven Galloway's remarkable new novel, *The Cellist of Sarajevo*, is . . . a glittering testament to the power of art to counteract hatred and division. . . . Galloway's novel, bursting with life, is a vivid reminder of the power of art to dispel the darkness."   —*The Vancouver Sun*

the
cellist
of
sarajevo

STEVEN GALLOWAY

RIVERHEAD BOOKS

New York

Riverhead Books
An imprint of Penguin Random House LLC
375 Hudson Street
New York, New York 10014

The Library of Congress has catalogued the Riverhead hardcover edition as follows:

Galloway, Steven.
    The cellist of Sarajevo / Steven Galloway.
       p.   cm.
    ISBN 9781594489860
    1. Sarajevo (Bosnia and Hercegovina)—Fiction.   2. Yugoslav War, 1991–1995—
Fiction.   3. Violoncellists—Fiction.   4. Snipers—Fiction.   I. Title.
    PR9199.3.G265C45   2008   2008000603
    813'.6—dc22

First Riverhead hardcover edition: May 2008
First Riverhead trade paperback edition: April 2009
Riverhead trade paperback ISBN: 9781594483653

Printed in the United States of America
33rd Printing

Cover design by Benjamin Gibson
Book design by Nicole Laroche

For Lara

The Sarajevo in this novel is only one small part of the real city and its people, as imagined by the author. This is above all else a work of fiction.

You may not be interested in war, but war is interested in you.

—LEON TROTSKY

the
  cellist
of
  sarajevo

the cellist

It screamed downward, splitting air and sky without effort. A target expanded in size, brought into focus by time and velocity. There was a moment before impact that was the last instant of things as they were. Then the visible world exploded.

In 1945, an Italian musicologist found four bars of a sonata's bass line in the remnants of the firebombed Dresden Music Library. He believed these notes were the work of the seventeenth-century Venetian composer Tomaso Albinoni, and spent the next twelve years reconstructing a larger piece from the charred manuscript fragment. The resulting composition, known as Albinoni's Adagio, bears little resemblance to most of Albinoni's work and is considered fraudulent by most scholars. But even those who doubt its authenticity have difficulty denying the Adagio's beauty.

Nearly half a century later, it's this contradiction that appeals to the cellist. That something could be almost erased from existence in the landscape of a ruined city, and then rebuilt until it is new and worthwhile, gives him hope. A hope that, now, is one of a limited number of things remaining for the besieged citizens of Sarajevo and that, for many, dwindles each day.

And so today, like every other day in recent memory, the cellist sits beside the window of his second-floor apartment and plays until he feels his hope return. He rarely plays the Adagio. Most days he's able to feel the music rejuvenate him as simply as if he were filling a car with gasoline. But some days this isn't the case. If, after several hours, this hope doesn't return, he will pause to gather himself, and then he and his cello will coax Albinoni's Adagio out of the firebombed husk of Dresden and into the mortar-pocked, sniper-infested streets of Sarajevo. By the time the last few notes fade, his hope will be restored, but each time he's forced to resort to the Adagio it becomes harder, and he knows its effect is finite. There are only a certain number of Adagios left in him, and he will not recklessly spend this precious currency.

It wasn't always like this. Not long ago the promise of a happy life seemed almost inviolable. Five years ago, at his sister's wedding, he'd posed for a family photograph, his father's arm slung behind his neck, fingers grasping his shoulder. It was a firm grip, and to some it would have been painful, but to the cellist it was the opposite. The fingers on his flesh told him that he was loved, that he had always been loved, and that the world was a place where above all else the things that were good would find a way to burrow into you. Though he knew all of this then, he would give up nearly anything to be able to go back in time and slow down that moment, if only so he could more clearly recall it now. He would very much like to feel his father's hand on his shoulder again.

He can tell today won't be an Adagio day. It has been only a half hour since he sat down beside the window, but already he feels a little bit better. Outside, a line of people wait to buy bread. It's been over a week since the market's had any bread to buy, and he considers whether he might join them. Many of his friends and neighbors are in line. He decides against it, for now. There's still work to do.

It screamed downward, splitting air and sky without effort. A target expanded in size, brought into focus by time and velocity. There was a moment before impact that was the last instant of things as they were. Then the visible world exploded.

When the mortars destroyed the Sarajevo Opera Hall, the cellist felt as if he were inside the building, as if the bricks and glass that once bound the structure together had become projectiles that sliced and pounded into him, shredding him beyond recognition. He was the principal cellist of the Sarajevo Symphony Orchestra. That was what he knew how to be. He made the idea of music an actuality. When he stepped onstage in his tuxedo he was transformed into an instrument of deliverance. He gave to the people who came to listen what he loved most in the world. He was as solid as the vise of his father's hand.

Now he doesn't care whether anyone hears him play or not. His tuxedo hangs in the closet, untouched. The guns perched on the hills surrounding Sarajevo have dismantled him just as they have the Opera Hall, just as they have his family home in the night while his father and mother slept, just as they will, eventually, everything.

The geography of the siege is simple. Sarajevo is a long ribbon of flat land surrounded on all sides by hills. The men on the hills control all the high ground and one peninsula of level ground in the middle of the city, Grbavica. They fire bullets and mortars and tank shells and grenades into the rest of the city, which is being defended by one tank and small handheld weapons. The city is being destroyed.

The cellist doesn't know what is about to happen. Initially the impact of the shell won't even register. For a long time he'll stand at his window and stare. Through the carnage and confusion he'll notice a woman's handbag, soaked in blood and sparkled with broken glass. He won't be able to tell whom it belongs to. Then he'll look down and see he has dropped his bow on the floor, and somehow it will seem to him that there's a great connection between these two objects. He won't understand what the connection is, but the feeling that it exists will compel him to undress, walk to the closet, and pull the dry cleaner's plastic from his tuxedo.

He will stand at the window all night and all through the next day. Then, at four o'clock in the afternoon, twenty-four hours after the mortar fell on his friends and neighbors while they waited to buy bread, he will bend down and pick up his bow. He will carry his cello and stool down the narrow flight of stairs to the empty street. The war will go on around him as he sits in the small crater left at the mortar's point of impact. He'll play Albinoni's Adagio. He'll do this every day for twenty-two days, a day for each person killed. Or at least he'll try. He won't be sure he will survive. He won't be sure he has enough Adagios left.

The cellist doesn't know any of this now, as he sits at his window in the sun and plays. He isn't yet aware. But it's already on its way. It screams downward, splitting air and sky without effort. A target expands in size, brought into focus by time and velocity. There is a moment before impact that is the last instant of things as they are. Then the visible world explodes.

one

arrow

Arrow blinks. She has been waiting for a long time. Through the scope of her rifle she can see three soldiers standing beside a low wall on a hill above Sarajevo. One looks at the city as though he's remembering something. One holds out a lighter so another can light a cigarette. It's obvious they have no idea they're in her sights. Perhaps, she thinks, they believe they're too far from the front line. They're wrong. Perhaps they think no one could thread a bullet between the buildings that separate them from her. Again, they're wrong. She can kill any one of them, and maybe even two of them, whenever she chooses. And soon she'll make her choice.

The soldiers Arrow is watching have good reason to think they're safe. Were almost anyone else hunting them, they would be. They're almost a kilometer away, and the rifle she uses, the kind nearly all the defenders use, has a practical range of eight hundred meters. Beyond that, the chances of hitting a target are remote. This isn't the case for Arrow. She can make a bullet do things that others can't.

For most people, long-distance shooting is a question of the correct combination of observation and mathematics. Figure out the wind's speed and direction, and the target's distance. Measurements are calculated and factored into equations taking into account the velocity of the bullet, the drop over time, the magnification of the scope. It's no different from throwing a ball. A ball isn't thrown at a target, it's thrown in an arc calculated to intersect with a target. Arrow doesn't take measurements, she doesn't calculate formulas. She simply sends the bullet where she knows it needs to go. She has trouble understanding why other snipers can't do this.

She's hidden among the detritus of a burned-out office tower, a few meters back from a window with a view of the city's southern hills. Anyone looking would have a difficult if not impossible time spotting a slight young woman with shoulder-length black hair concealed within the smoking wreckage of workaday life. She lies with her stomach pressed to the floor, her legs partially covered by an old newspaper. Her eyes, large, blue, and bright, are the only sign of life.

Arrow believes she's different from the snipers on the hills. She shoots only soldiers. They shoot unarmed men, women, children. When they kill a person, they seek a result that is far greater than the elimination of that individual. They are trying to kill the city. Every death chips away at the Sarajevo of Arrow's youth with as much certainty as any mortar shell battering a building. Those left are robbed of not only a fellow citizen but the memory of what it was to be alive in a time before men on the hills shot at you while you tried to cross the street.

Ten years ago, when she was eighteen and was not called Arrow, she borrowed her father's car and drove to the countryside to visit friends. It was a bright, clear day, and the car felt alive to her, as though the way she and the car moved together was a sort of destiny, and everything was happening exactly as it ought to. As she rounded a corner one of her favorite songs came on the radio, and sunlight filtered through the trees the way it does with lace curtains, reminding her of her grandmother, and tears began to slide down her cheeks. Not for her grandmother, who was then still very much among the living, but because she felt an enveloping happiness to be alive, a joy made stronger by the certainty that someday it would all come to an end. It overwhelmed her, made her pull the car to the side of the road. Afterward she felt a little foolish, and never spoke to anyone about it.

Now, however, she knows she wasn't being foolish. She realizes that for no particular reason she stumbled into the core of what it is to be human. It's a rare gift to understand that your life is wondrous, and that it won't last forever.

So when Arrow pulls the trigger and ends the life of one of the soldiers in her sights, she'll do so not because she wants him dead, although she can't deny that she does, but because the soldiers have robbed her and almost everyone else in the city of this gift. That life will end has become so self-evident it's lost all meaning. But worse, for Arrow, is the damage done to the distance between what she knows and what she believes. For although she knows her tears that day were not the ridiculous sentimentality of a teenage girl, she doesn't really believe it.

From the elevated fortress of Vraca, above the occupied neighborhood of Grbavica, her targets bomb the city with assumed impunity. In the Second World War, Vraca was a place where the Nazis tortured and killed those who resisted them. The names of the dead are carved on the steps, but at the time few fighters used their real names. They took new names, names that said more about them than any boastful story told by drunks in a bar, names that defied the governments who later tried to twist their deeds into propaganda. It's said they took these new names so their families wouldn't be in danger, so they could slip in and out of two lives. But Arrow believes they took these names so they could separate themselves from what they had to do, so the person who fought and killed could someday be put away. To hate people because they hated her first, and then to hate them because of what they've done to her, has created a desire to separate the part of her that will fight back, that will enjoy fighting back, from the part that never wanted to fight in the first place. Using her real name would make her no different from the men she kills. It would be a death greater than the end of her life.

From the first time she picked up a rifle to kill she has called herself Arrow. There are some who continue to call her by her former name. She ignores them. If they persist, she tells them her name is Arrow now. No one argues. No one questions what she must do. Everyone does something to stay alive. But if they were to press her, she would say, "I am Arrow, because I hate them. The woman you knew hated nobody."

Arrow has chosen today's targets because she doesn't want the men at Vraca to feel safe. She will have to make an extremely difficult shot. Though she hides on the ninth floor of this depredated building, the fortress is an uphill run, and she must slip the bullet between a series of buildings that stand between her and her target. The soldiers must stay within a space of about three meters, and smoke from burning buildings periodically obscures her view. As soon as she lets off a shot, every sniper on the southern hill will begin to search for her. They'll quickly figure out where she is. At that point they'll shell the building, into the ground if necessary. And the reason this building is burned out is that it's an easy target. Her chances of escaping the repercussions of her own bullets are slim. But this isn't an unusual set of challenges. She has sent bullets through trickier air and faced swifter retaliation in the past.

Arrow knows exactly how long it will take them to locate her. She knows exactly where the snipers will look and exactly where the mortars will hit. By the time the shelling stops she'll be gone, though none will understand how, even those on her own side defending the city. If she told them they wouldn't understand. They wouldn't believe that she knows what a weapon will do because Arrow herself is a weapon. She possesses a particular kind of genius few would want to accept. If she could choose, she wouldn't believe in it either. But she knows it isn't up to her. You don't choose what to believe. Belief chooses you.

One of the three soldiers moves away from the other two. Arrow tenses, waiting to see if the two salute him. If they do she will fire. For a moment she's unsure, unable to read their gestures. Then the soldier steps out of the narrow corridor her bullet can travel through. He has, in an instant of seeming inconsequence, saved his life. A life is composed almost entirely of actions like this, Arrow knows.

She watches them a while longer, waiting for a detail to emerge that will dictate which one receives the first bullet. She wants to fire twice, to kill both of them, but she isn't confident there will be that opportunity, and if she must choose just one of the soldiers she would like to make the right choice, if there's a right choice to be made. Ultimately she doesn't believe it will make much difference. Perhaps one of them will live, but he'll never understand how slim the margin of his existence is. He will chalk it up to luck, or fate, or merit. He'll never know that an arbitrary fraction of a millimeter in her aim one way or another will make the difference between feeling the sun on his face ten minutes from now and looking down to see an unbelievable hole in his chest feeling all he was or could have become drain out of him, and then, in his final moments, inhaling more pain than he knew the world could hold.

One of the soldiers says something and laughs. The other one joins in, but from the tightness in his mouth it seems to Arrow that his laugh is perhaps only for his companion's benefit. She ponders this. Does she shoot the instigator or the collaborator? She's not sure. For the next few minutes she watches the two men smoke and talk. Their hands trace hard shapes through the air, physical punctuation, sometimes pausing, like knives poised in anticipation of a strike. They're both young, younger than she is, and if she wished herself into ignorance she could almost imagine they were discussing the outcome of a recent football match. Perhaps, she thinks, they are. It's possible, even likely, that they view this as some sort of game. Boys throwing bombs instead of balls.

Then they both turn their heads as though called by someone Arrow can't see, and she knows the time to fire has come. Nothing has made a decision for her, so Arrow simply chooses one. If there's a reason, if it's because one shot is easier, or one of them reminds her of someone she once knew and liked or didn't like, or one of them seems more dangerous than the other, she can't say. The only certainty is that she exhales and her finger goes from resting on the trigger to squeezing it, and a bullet breaks the sound barrier an instant before pulping fabric, skin, bone, flesh, and organ, beginning a short process that will turn motion into meat.

As Arrow readies her second shot, in the time between the tick of one second and another, she knows that something has gone wrong. The men on the hills know where she is. She abandons her shot and rolls to the side, aware of eyes upon her, that a sniper has been hunting her all along, and the instant she shot she was exposed. They have set a trap for her and she has fallen into it. A bullet hits the floor where she lay an instant before. As she scuttles toward the skeleton of a staircase that will lead her nine flights down and out of the building she hears a rifle fire, but doesn't hear the bullet strike. This means either the sniper has missed entirely or she has been hit. She doesn't feel any pain, though she's heard you don't at first. There isn't any need to check if she's hit. If a bullet has found her she'll know soon enough.

Arrow enters the stairwell and a mortar comes through the roof and explodes. She's two flights down when another lands, sending the ninth floor crumbling into the eighth. As she reaches the sixth floor the texture of the situation shifts in her mind, and she veers into a dark, narrow hallway and moves as quickly as she can away from the mortar she knows is about to penetrate the stairwell. She manages to make it far enough to avoid the steel and wood and concrete the explosion sends her, a multitude of bullets as interest paid on the loan of one. But then, as the last piece of shrapnel hits the ground, she turns and runs back toward the staircase. She has no choice. There's no other way out of this building, and if she stays she will collect on her loan. So she returns to the stairwell, not knowing what remains of it. The sixth floor has collapsed into the fifth, and when she jumps to the landing below she wonders if it will bear her. It does, and from there it's a matter of staying tight against the inner wall where the stairs meet the building, where the weight of the upper layers of the collapsed stairway has had less impact.

Arrow hears another mortar hit as she reaches the ground, and although the front entrance leading to the street is only steps away she continues to the basement, where she feels her way along a dim corridor until she finds a door. She shoulders it open. The immediate shift from darkness to light momentarily blinds her, but she emerges without hesitation into a low stairwell on the north side of the building, somewhat sheltered from the men on the southern hill. Before her eyes adjust to the world around her she begins to notice the percussion of mortars affecting her hearing, and it reminds her of being in a swimming pool, of a day when she and a friend took turns shouting each other's names underwater and laughing at how they came out, all garbled and distorted and foreign. When she turns east, away from the building, she feels a pain in her side, and she looks down, half expecting to see her stomach distended between splintered ribs. A quick inspection reveals only a slight cut, a small nothing that attached itself to her at some point during her exit.

As she walks toward her unit's headquarters in the city

center, she notices that the sky is beginning to darken. A few drops of rain hit her forehead, make her feel her own heat as they evaporate. When she touches her side, her hand comes away without any fresh blood on it, and Arrow wonders what it means that the insignificance of her injury does not bring her any particular sense of relief.

kenan

Another day has just begun. Light strains its way into the apartment, where it finds Kenan in his kitchen, his hand reaching for the plastic jug containing his family's final quarter-liter of water. His movement is slow and stiff. He seems to himself more an old man than one who will soon celebrate his fortieth birthday. His wife, Amila, who is sleeping in the sitting room because it's more secure than their street-facing bedroom, is much the same. Like him, her middle age has somehow escaped her. She's barely thirty-seven, but looks well over fifty. Her hair is thin and her skin hangs loose off her flesh, suggesting a former woman who, Kenan knows, never was.

At least their children are, for now, still children. Like all children they rail against the limitations placed on them, and they want to be grown-up, and they wish things to be other than they are. They know what's going on, but they don't entirely understand. They have learned how to live with it. Perhaps, Kenan suspects, that's why they don't turn old.

It has been over a month since the last time the family had

electricity for more than a few hours, and even longer without running water. While life is more difficult without electricity, it is impossible without water. So every four days Kenan gathers his collection of plastic containers and travels down the hill, through the old town, across the Miljacka River and up into the hills into Stari Grad, to the brewery, one of the only places in the city where a person can get clean drinking water. Occasionally it is possible to find closer sources of water, and he keeps his eye out for them, but they're unreliable and often unsafe. He doesn't want to survive the men on the hills only to be killed by a waterborne parasite, a possibility he considers real and pressing in a city that no longer has a functioning sewage system. The brewery's water comes from underground springs deep in the water table, and he feels this is well worth the risk of the extra distance.

As quietly as he can, Kenan picks up the final jug of water and moves down the hall toward the bathroom. His hand flicks on the light switch, a leftover reflex from earlier times. The bulb in the ceiling surges to life. Kenan strikes a match, lights the stub of a candle that sits on the side of the sink below the mirror. He puts the stopper in the drain and pours his quarter-liter of water into the sink. He wets his face, blinks as the cold water registers in his mind as shock. His hands work a small bar of soap into a lather he applies to his cheeks, neck, chin, and upper lip. The razor settles into a rhythmic scratch scratch splash, his pupils narrowing in the light as he observes his progress. When he's done he wets his face again and dries himself on a crusty towel hanging above the toilet. He blows out the candle and is surprised when light does not disappear from the room. After a few seconds he realizes that the electricity is on, that the bulb above his head is glowing, and he almost smiles at his mistake before he understands the significance of it. He has grown accustomed to a world where you shave by candlelight with soap and cold water. It has become normal.

Still, there is electricity, and because that is no longer normal he rushes out of the bathroom to wake his wife, who will want to get the children up to make the most of it. He imagines a breakfast cooked on the stove, and watching the television next to the warmth of the heater. The children's excitement will be catching as they laugh at one of their cartoons. Light will fill all of the rooms and chase away the perpetual dusk that hides in the corners. Even if it doesn't last for long it will make them happy, and for the rest of the day their faces will be tired from smiling. But as he leaves the room he hears a telltale pop, and when he looks back the light is off. He tries the hall light and confirms what he already knows to be true. He returns to the kitchen. There's no longer any reason to wake his family.

He sits at the table and inspects each of the six plastic containers he'll take with him. He checks for any obvious cracks that may have developed since they were last emptied, makes sure each one has the correct lid. He has two backup containers he can substitute if he finds any faults. Deciding how much water you can carry has become something of an art in this city. Carry too little and you'll have to repeat the task more often. Each time you expose yourself to the dangers of the streets you run the risk of injury or death. But carry too much and you lose the ability to run, duck, dive, anything it takes to get out of danger's way. Kenan has decided on eight canisters. The six from his house will hold about twenty-four liters of water. Two more will come from Mrs. Ristovski, the elderly neighbor downstairs.

As he verifies that his six containers are reliable, he hears his wife rise from her bed. She leans into the doorway of the kitchen, rubs sleep from her eyes.

"It was quiet last night," he says. "It won't be too bad out there today."

She nods. They both know a quiet night in no way means it will be a quiet day, but Kenan is glad that neither says so.

His wife moves across the room and stands in front of him. She places her hand on his head, resting it there before letting it slide down to his shoulder, giving his ear a light tug on its way. "Be careful."

Kenan smiles. It's not so much her words that bring him comfort but that she still says them. She knows as well as he that there's no such thing as careful, that the men on the hills can kill anyone, anywhere, any time they like, and that luck or fate or whatever it is that decides who lives and who doesn't has not, in the past, favored those who act in a way that could be described as careful. The odds may punish those who behave recklessly, but everyone else seems about even. Still, there was a time when a person could reasonably act with care for his well-being, and he appreciates that his wife is occasionally willing, for the sake of his sanity, to invoke the memory of those times.

He sees her looking at his bottles, tallying them up. "Mrs. Ristovski?"

"Yes."

She frowns, brushes a strand of hair out of her eyes. Then her face softens, and she stands back to look at him. "You'll need a new coat soon."

"I'll pick one up while I'm out," he says. "Would you like me to get you some shoes?"

She smiles. Kenan grins back. He's glad that he can still make her smile. "No," she says, "but I'll take a hat if you have time."

"Of course," he says. "I assume you would like mink?"

The children are awake now, and she kisses him quick on the cheek before going to check on them. "You should go, before you see them and lose an hour with your jokes."

As the door to his apartment closes behind him he presses his back to it and slides to the ground. His legs are heavy, his hands cold. He doesn't want to go. What he wants is to go back inside, crawl into bed, and sleep until this war is over. He wants to take his younger daughter to a carnival. He wants to sit up, anxious, waiting for his older daughter to return from a movie with a boy he doesn't really like. He wants his son, the middle child, only ten years old, to think about anything other than how long it will be before he can join the army and fight.

Muffled sounds seep out of the apartment, and he worries that one of the children might come to the door. They must not see him like this. They must not know how afraid he is, how useless he is, how powerless he has become. If he doesn't return home today he doesn't want them to remember him sitting on the landing, shaking like a wet and frightened dog.

He pushes himself to his feet and picks up the water containers. He's tied them together by the handles with a piece of rope, and although bulky they're light and easy enough to carry while empty. Later, when they're full, it will be harder, but he'll deal with that then. Kenan knows he's getting progressively weaker, like almost everyone else in the city, and wonders if the day will come when he won't be able to carry back enough water for his family. What then? Will he have to take his son along on the trip, as many others do? He doesn't want to do that. If he is killed he doesn't want anyone in his family to witness it, as much as he would like their faces to be the last thing he sees. And if both he and his son were killed he knows his wife would never recover. If he thinks about what might happen if his son alone died he'll be back down on the ground.

He descends the flight of stairs that leads to the ground floor and knocks on the door to Mrs. Ristovski's apartment. Hearing no sounds of movement inside, he knocks again with more force. He hears a shuffling and waits for the door to open.

Mrs. Ristovski has lived in this building nearly her whole life, or so she says. Given that she's well into her seventies and it was built shortly after the Second World War, Kenan knows that this can't be true, but he isn't inclined to argue. Mrs. Ristovski believes what she believes, and no mere facts will convince her otherwise.

When Kenan and his wife first moved into the building their older daughter had just been born. Mrs. Ristovski complained constantly about the child's crying, and as new parents they listened to her criticisms and advice, deferring to the wisdom of someone older and more experienced. After a while, however, they decided that it wasn't the crying that was bothering her. Kenan began to suspect that the baby had become a focal point for all her discontent. Though annoyed by her repeated intrusions into their lives, Kenan tolerated Mrs. Ristovski, often above his wife's objections. There was something about her ferocity that he admired, even if he didn't quite like it.

After the war started, Mrs. Ristovski knocked on their door and, when Kenan opened it, pushed her way past him. His wife was out, but Mrs. Ristovski didn't appear to notice. She sat on the sofa in the front room while he made coffee. He put the coffee on a silver tray and placed it on the low table in front of her, but she didn't touch it.

"Do you have any brandy?" she asked, straightening the tray.

"Of course," he said. He poured each of them a generous measure.

Mrs. Ristovski downed her glass in one swallow. Kenan watched the color rise in her corrugated neck, then fade away.

"Well," she said, "this will be the end of me."

"What will?" he asked, thinking she was referring to the brandy.

"This war." She looked him in the eye. He did his best not to stare at the large mole on the side of her face, tried not to wonder if it was getting bigger. She shook her head. "You've never lived through a war. You have no idea what it will be like."

"It won't last long," he said. "The rest of Europe will do something to stop it from escalating."

She snorted. "That won't matter for me. I'm too old to do the things one must do in wartime to survive."

Kenan wasn't sure what she meant. He knew that she had been married just before the last war and that her husband was killed during the initial days of the German invasion. "It might not be that bad," he said, regretting it immediately, knowing it wasn't true.

"You have no idea," she repeated.

"Well," he said, "I will help you. Everyone in the building will help each other. You'll see."

Mrs. Ristovski picked up her coffee and took a sip. She didn't look at Kenan, refusing to acknowledge his smile. "We'll see," she said.

A few weeks later, after the men on the hills shut off the city's water supply, she showed up at his door as he was preparing to embark on his first trip to the brewery. In her hands were two plastic bottles. She pushed them at him. "A promise is a promise," she said. Then she turned and went back to her apartment, leaving a dumbfounded Kenan standing in the doorway. But he could not refuse her. No person he would want to be would do that.

The door to Mrs. Ristovski's apartment opens a crack, just enough for her to see out. "What? It's early."

"I'm going for water." He isn't going to play her games. It's common knowledge that she rises with the sun. She's likely been up for an hour or two, and Kenan can recall at least a half-dozen instances in recent months when she's knocked on his door earlier than this.

The door closes. "Mrs. Ristovski? I'm not going again for at least a few days."

He hears her banging around inside, muttering curses, and then the door opens again, wider this time. She thrusts her two water bottles at him, shaking them when he is slow to take them from her.

Kenan looks at the bottles. "These don't have handles." They're the kind that soft drinks come in, holding two liters each. He's been asking her for weeks to switch to some with handles, so that he can tie them to his own containers. He's even offered to give her two of his own, his backups.

"This is how much water I need. If I switch to different ones I might not get enough."

"The other ones are larger." He holds them out to her, but she doesn't take them.

"You're not a human measuring cup," she says as she closes the door.

Kenan stands in the foyer and listens to the sound of the door echo up the stairwell. He thinks about leaving her bottles outside her door, of just giving up on her. Surely she wouldn't die if she went a few days without water. It might teach her a lesson. It's a pleasing but pointless thought. As much as he might regret it, she was right, he made her a promise. He looks at the plastic bottles in his hands, shakes his head, pushes open the door to his building, and steps out into the street.

dragan

There is no way to tell which version of a lie is the truth. Now, after all that has happened, Dragan knows that the Sarajevo he remembers, the city he grew up in and was proud of and happy with, likely never existed. If he looks around him, it's hard to see what once was, or maybe was. More and more it seems like there has never been anything here but the men on the hills with guns and bombs. Somehow that doesn't seem right either, yet these are the only two options.

This is what Dragan remembers of Sarajevo. Steep mountains receded into a valley. On the flat of the valley, the Miljacka River cut the city in half lengthwise, from tip to tail. On the left bank, the southern hills led up to Mount Trebević, where some of the alpine events for the 1984 Winter Olympics were held. If you went west you would see neighborhoods like Stari Grad, Grbavica, Novi Grad, Mojmilo, Dobrinja, and, finally, Ilidža, where there was a park filled with trees, streams, and a pond where swans lived in what looked like a dog's house. You would pass by the Academy of Fine Arts, the sporting and trade complex of Skenderija, the Grbavica football stadium, the Palma pastry shop, the offices of the newspaper *Oslobođenje*, the airport, and the Butmir settlement, where Neolithic humans lived five thousand years ago.

If you then went north, across the river, and headed back the way you came, along the right bank to the east, you would go through neighborhoods like Halilovići, Novo Sarajevo, Marind-vor, Koševo, Bjelave, and Baščaršija. You could have ridden the streetcar, which ran down the middle of the main street until it reached the old part of the city. There it formed a loop, west along the river, past the Parliament Building, the Sarajevo Canton Building, the post office, the theater, the university, and then, at the old town hall where the library was housed, curved up and around, back past the Markale marketplace and Veliki Park until it reunited with the main line. Here you could go north, to Koševo Stadium, where the opening and closing cer-emonies of the Olympic Games were held, or to the hospital, which was just across the street.

Sarajevo was a great city for walking. It was impossible to get lost. If you didn't know where you were, you just went downhill until you hit the river, and from there it would all be obvious. If you got tired you could sit in a café and have a coffee, or, if you were hungry, stop at a small restaurant for a meat pie. People were happy. Life was good. This is, at least, how Dragan remembers it. It could be, he thinks, that it is all a figment of his imagination. Now, he knows, you can't walk from one end of the city to the other. Grbavica is entirely controlled by the men on the hills, and even to go near it would be suicide. The same is true of Ilidža. Dobrinja, though it has not fallen, is often cut off from the rest of the city, and is, like most places, extraordinarily dangerous. Skenderija is a smoldering ruin. So are the post office, the Parliament and Canton buildings, *Oslobođenje*, and the library. Koševo Stadium has burned to the ground, and its fields are being used to bury the dead. The trains don't run anymore. The streets are full of debris, boxcars and concrete piled at intersections in an attempt to foil the snipers on the hills. To go outside is to accept the possibility you will be killed. On the other hand, Dragan knows, the same can be said of staying inside.

Every day the Sarajevo he thinks he remembers slips away from him a little at a time, like water cupped in the palms of his hands, and when it's gone he wonders what will be left. He isn't sure what it will be like to live without remembering how life used to be, what it was like to live in a beautiful city. When the war first started he tried to fight the loss of the city, tried to keep what he could intact. When he looked at a building, he'd try to see it as it had once been, and when he looked at someone he knew, he tried to ignore the changes in their appearance and behavior. But as time went on he began to see things as they now were, and then one day he knew that he was no longer fighting the city's disappearance, even in his mind. What he saw around him was his only reality.

He has been on the streets for about an hour today, trying to make his way west from where he lives in the middle of town, just up the hill from the outdoor market. He's trying to get to the city's bakery, where he works. He has worked at the bakery for almost forty years, and were it not for the war he would likely be contemplating retirement. Dragan knows he's extremely fortunate to have this job and the exemption from forced military service that comes with it, although even an exemption means little to the gangs of thugs searching for new conscripts. Nearly everyone in the city is now unemployed, and even though he rarely gets paid in cash, which is more or less useless anyway, he's paid in bread to take home, and if he goes to the employee cafeteria he can eat for free, whether he's working or not. So even though he isn't working today, he's on his way to the bakery to eat, because if he eats there he won't have to eat at home.

Home is a three-room apartment in Mejtaš, north of the old town, shared with his younger sister and her family. Dragan used to live in what he considered a very nice apartment in the neighborhood of Hrasno, just to the west of Grbavica. Now it's on the front line of the fighting. The last time he saw it a grenade had completely destroyed the interior of the apartment, and he's pretty sure that since then the entire building has collapsed. Either way, it wasn't possible to stay there, and he knows he won't ever go back.

Dragan managed to get his wife, Raza, and their eighteen-year-old son out of the city before the war started, and they are, he thinks, in Italy now. He hasn't heard from them in three months and has no idea when he will get word from them again. A part of him doesn't want to hear from them until the war is over. He has heard of women sending divorce papers from abroad, and he's not sure he could handle that. He's sixty-four, looks more like a grandfather than a father. While they never had the perfect marriage, it was a comfortable life for both of them, though she was six years younger than he and they'd had their son, Davor, late, when she was forty. They'd thought they couldn't have children.

He hopes that, wherever they are, his wife and son are happy. He's glad they don't have to share his sister's apartment. Dragan and his brother-in-law have never got along and, though neither will admit it, they would both prefer to spend much less time together than they do. But the bread Dragan brings home makes him indispensable, and the roof they put over his head traps him there.

The bakery isn't far from his sister's house, maybe three kilometers. Under normal conditions it would be about a forty-five-minute walk. Nowadays it takes an hour and a half if he hurries. Today he's mainly out for the sake of being out, though, and he's been taking his time. He's kept his pace slow almost the whole way, with the exception of the part of the main road that intersects with Vrbanja Bridge, an especially dangerous spot. There he ran across the street as quickly as he could, trying not to think about whether he was in someone's sights.

He's on the main road, the one where the streetcars used to run. The south side of the street is piled high in places with barriers to shield cars and pedestrians from the hills to the south, though there are still plenty of places for a sniper to sneak a bullet through. He's heard foreigners call this street Sniper Alley, and this makes him laugh, because it seems to him that every street in Sarajevo could have this name. Were the streets running along the banks of the Miljacka not worthy? What about every single part of Dobrinja or Mojmilo? It would be easier just to call every road in town Sniper Alley, and then, by some act of magnificence, if there was a street that was impenetrable to the men on the hills, to single that street out for a special name. But, of course, this is the road that takes the foreigners from the airport to the Holiday Inn, so it must seem particularly dangerous to them. Still, six lanes of pavement and a median for the trams hardly seems to Dragan like an alley.

He cuts north, leaving the main road, which, if he continues on it, will veer too close to enemy territory for his liking. This part of the street is heavily guarded by the defenders, but that has never stopped a sniper in the past and he has no illusions that it will stop one today.

He links up with another busy street, the preferred route for many people traveling the length of the city. As he reaches another main intersection, between Marshal Tito's Barracks and the Energoinvest Tower, both almost entirely destroyed, Dragan prepares to run. This is one of the most dangerous intersections in the city. Only four hundred meters to the south is the Brotherhood and Unity Bridge, which separates the right bank of the city from occupied Grbavica.

To his left there are eight boxcars, piled two high, lining the street. To his right are the railroad tracks. On the far side of the street is the Energoinvest Tower. A few years ago it was one of the city's largest high-rise office towers. Now it's in ruins, shelled out of existence. Everything around him is a peculiar shade of gray. He's not sure where it came from, if it was always there and the war has simply stripped away the color that hid it, or if this gray is the color of war. Either way, it gives the whole street a bleak feeling.

There are about twenty people waiting at the intersection to cross. Some step out and begin to run as though there's a rain-cloud over this part of the street and they don't want to get any wetter than necessary. It almost seems routine to these people. Or at least that's how it looks to Dragan. There are others who hover for a second and then run as fast as they can until they reach the other side. They make this brief frenetic dash and then keep walking as though nothing has happened.

Dragan is one of those who waits behind the protection of a concrete wall for a sign or a feeling that it's okay to cross. He's never quite sure what could possibly happen that might make a difference, but sooner or later he always feels that the time to cross has come. So far he's still alive, so he figures that whatever it is he's doing must be right.

Since the war began Dragan has seen three people killed by snipers. What surprised him the most was how quickly it all happens. One moment the people are walking or running through the street, and then they drop abruptly as though they were marionettes and their puppeteer has fainted. As they fall there's a sharp crack of gunfire, and everyone in the area seeks cover. After a few minutes, though, things seem to go back to what they now call normal. The bodies are recovered, if possible, and the wounded are taken away. No one has any way of knowing if the sniper who fired is still there or if he has moved, but everyone behaves as though he has gone until the next time he fires, and then the cycle repeats itself. It doesn't appear to Dragan to make much difference whether the shot hits or misses. It may have in the beginning, months and months ago, but not now. Now people are used to seeing other people being shot in the street.

Of the three people Dragan has seen killed, two were hit in the head and died immediately. One was hit in the chest and then, about a minute later, the neck. It was a much worse death. Dragan is afraid of dying, but what he's afraid of more is the time that might come between being shot and dying. He isn't sure how long it takes to die when you're shot in the head, if it's instantaneous or if your consciousness remains for a few seconds, and he's skeptical of anyone who claims to know for certain. Either way, it's a lot better than gulping air like a fish in the bottom of a boat, watching your own blood gush into the ground and thinking whatever thoughts people have when they see themselves ending.

He's reached the intersection and can't go any further without exposing himself to the hills. There's a small group of people milling at the edge of the street, none of them crossing, none of them turning back. They all watch as a man on the other side begins to cross. He hunches a bit as he runs, a cigarette hanging from his lips. Dragan recognizes this man. His name is Amil and he works, or used to work, at the news kiosk outside Dragan's old building. Dragan hasn't seen him since the war started, hasn't even thought about him.

As Amil reaches the other side, he stops running and puts his hands in the pockets of his jeans. The collar of his leather jacket is flipped up on one side, and his hair is shorter than Dragan remembers it being. Amil is only a few meters from him and if he looks up he'll see him. Dragan turns and faces the wall behind him, as though examining it, and waits until Amil passes. It doesn't seem as though Amil noticed him.

When he's gone, Dragan thinks about what he's just done and feels momentarily guilty. He always liked Amil, used to talk to him all the time. But that was before the war. If they were to speak now they would both be reminded only of how much has been lost, how things are no longer what they once were. And even though there's nowhere in the city Dragan could look that wouldn't tell him this same message, it's somehow more painful to see it in another human being, someone you once knew.

He's stopped talking to his friends, visits no one, avoids those who come to visit him. At work he says as little as possible. He can perhaps learn to bear the destruction of buildings, but the destruction of the living is too much for him. If people are going to be taken away from him, either through death or a transformation of their personality that makes them into strangers, then he's better off without them.

Ahead of him, a couple have decided it's time to cross. A man and a woman in their early thirties, he guesses. The woman is wearing a dress made of a floral fabric that reminds him of the curtains in the house he grew up in. They have been holding hands, and as they step into the street each lets go of the other's hand and begins to move more quickly, not quite running. When they're a third of the way across a bullet skids off the asphalt in front of the man, and Dragan hears the crisp smack of a rifle. The couple hesitate, not sure whether to turn back or keep going. Then the man makes a decision, and he grabs the woman's arm and pulls her toward him. They're running now, heading for the other side of the street. They're nearly there when the sniper fires again, but either they're lucky or the sniper makes a mistake, because their puppeteer remains standing and they reach the other side.

The people around him breathe easier, relieved, partly because the couple made it, and partly because they no longer have to wonder whether the intersection is being targeted today. There's a strange sense of relief in knowing where the danger is. It's much easier to deal with than an unfocused sense of doom, of being uncertain about where the men on the hills are shooting. At least now they know. For a few minutes no one ventures into the street, but Dragan knows that eventually someone will risk it, and then someone else, until everyone who was here when the sniper fired is gone, and those who arrive won't even know about the couple's narrow escape. The sniper will fire again, though, if not here then somewhere else, and if not him then someone else, and it will all happen again, like a herd of gazelle going back to the water hole after one of their own is eaten there.

two

kenan

The walk downhill toward the old town would have begun Kenan's day whether the war was on or not. Until recently he worked as a clerical assistant in an accounting firm, but the building is now destroyed, and in any case there's no work to do. If he makes a great effort, however, if he controls what he sees and thinks, if he forgets about the water bottles he's carrying, he can, for the first few blocks, fool himself into imagining that he's on his way to work. Perhaps he'll have lunch with one of his colleagues. Perhaps they'll sit outside in Veliki Park with a coffee. He might tease his friend Goran, who is, inexplicably, a fan of the Chelsea Football Club, about a recent loss.

Soon, though, he will arrive at a switchback where the neighborhood trash bins are located. They're no longer visible beneath an ever-growing heap of refuse which is scoured daily for anything of the slightest value. As soon as he sees this he can no longer ignore the overturned cars or the buildings with their innards exposed. He can't help hearing gunfire in the distance, and he remembers that Veliki Park is one of the most dangerous parts of the city. He hasn't seen Goran for months, and suspects he's dead.

He continues downhill. If he looks up he can see the mountains to the south. He wonders if the men on the hills can see him. He imagines it's possible. Any decent pair of binoculars would reveal him, a thin, youngish man in a shabby brown coat, carrying two bouquets of plastic bottles. They could kill him now, he supposes. But then again, they could have killed him any one of a number of times already, and if they don't kill him now they'll have more opportunities in the future. He doesn't know why some people die and others don't. He doesn't have any idea how the men on the hills make their choices, and he doesn't think he wants to know. What would he think about it? Would he be flattered they didn't choose him or offended he wasn't a worthy target in their eyes?

Kenan is flanked on either side by four- and five-storey apartment buildings. None of them has escaped damage, though this neighborhood has fared far better than many others in the city. Beside him is a green Volkswagen sedan that has been hit by a shell. It looks as if an enormous thumb has pressed into it, as though it were made of dough. The windshield has been blown out, and the driver's-side door has been ripped apart. Kenan thinks the car belongs to a man who lives on the second floor of the building across the street. It's hard to tell. The man didn't mention his car being destroyed the last time Kenan saw him, but that's no longer the sort of thing one mentions.

On his left is the relief center, housed on the ground floor of a postwar walk-up, in what used to be a grocery market. The doors are closed, but he approaches, hoping there might be some information about when the next relief convoy is expected. Often they post up notices about what goods will be available, so people know what kinds of bags and containers to bring with them. As he gets closer he sees there is no poster. It has been weeks since the last aid, maybe over a month.

He turns back to the street and sees a man he knows, a soldier. Ismet smiles, changes direction, and comes toward him. They're about the same age and have been friends for over a decade. When the war started, Ismet was one of the first to join the army. He worked as a taxi driver before the war, but his car was destroyed, and now he walks nearly eight kilometers to the front lines in the north, by the television relay station. He usually spends four days at the front and then returns home for four days, to be with his wife and infant daughter. Sometimes, late at night, he comes to Kenan's house and tells him about the fighting. He has told him of sharing a gun with another man, how they had twenty bullets, how it was their job to stop three tanks from advancing along a ridge. All the while they knew that if the tanks advanced there would be nothing they could do. Their bullets would be gone in an instant, and useless anyway. They spent the entire night in terror, flinching every time they heard a noise. When morning came, Ismet had never been so happy, nor had his friend. Later that day, as they slept in an improvised bunker slightly behind the lines, a shell landed a few meters from them, and Ismet's friend was killed. Ismet told Kenan all this without any expression on his face, but when he reached the end he smiled and laughed a little. When Kenan asked him why, Ismet looked at him as though he hadn't been listening. "We survived the night," he said. "That was all we had wished for. When we were given it and it made us happy. Whether we lived for another few hours or fifty more years didn't matter."

During moments like these Kenan wonders why he can't bring himself to join the army. So far he's managed to avoid being drafted, has kept clear of the men who drive through the city rounding up unwilling conscripts. He's safe while he has the water jugs, as no one is yet bold enough to interrupt this vital civilian mission. But he doesn't know how long this will last, how long it will be before there's a knock on his door and he ends up with a gun in his hands.

It's true that he's not a young man, though he's young enough. It's true that he's in poor physical condition, has three children to look after, and has no skills that are of use to an army. But they would take him. Men who are much older, have larger families, and are less suited to combat have enlisted. But Kenan hasn't. He knows the real reason.

He's afraid of dying. He may very well die at any time, whether he's in the army or not, but he feels that as a civilian his chances are lower, and if he's killed it will be unjust, whereas for a soldier death is part of the job. If he ends up in the army, he knows that sooner or later he will have to kill someone. And as afraid as he is of dying, he's more afraid of killing. He doesn't think he could do it. He knows he wants to, sometimes, and that there are men on the other side who certainly deserve to die, but he doesn't believe that he could perform the physical mechanics of it all. It takes courage to kill a man, and he doesn't possess such courage. A man who can barely leave his family to collect water without falling down outside the door could not possibly do what Ismet does.

Kenan isn't sure whether Ismet can sense this tension within him. He's never brought it up, never known quite how to, and as time passes, the fact that Ismet is fighting to save them all and Kenan is not has grown larger and larger.

Today Ismet looks particularly tired. His green jacket, with its insignia stitched on by his wife, is covered in mud, and he hasn't shaved in a while. Thanks to a recent wound, he walks with a slight limp, more noticeable because of his great height. His hair is longer than he usually wears it, but still the color of coal. The bags under his eyes remind Kenan of a hound, the kind that chases down escaped prisoners in movies.

The two men embrace, and Kenan is glad to see his friend. He doesn't want to admit it, but he has been expecting and dreading the day that Ismet doesn't come back. "How are things?"

Ismet grins. "They are as others want them." He gestures toward the relief center. "Any news?"

Kenan shakes his head. "I was hoping for some meat this time. Perhaps a nice steak, or a lamb." This is a running joke between them.

"Bah. You don't need that. If you want meat, eat a centipede. You'll get all the feet you can stomach." He pulls a pack of cigarettes from his pocket, offers it.

Kenan refuses. Though he'd like one, he knows Ismet probably has only this pack, maybe one other, given to him by the army instead of pay, and when they run out he'll feel it more. Kenan has given up smoking, viewing it as a luxury he can't afford, and he thinks he can stick with it.

"Go on, take it, don't be a martyr. It's not my last one." Ismet pulls a cigarette from the pack and thrusts it into Kenan's hand. "Do it as a favor to me."

The tobacco makes him a little light-headed, but it's good. He's missed this. "Thanks."

The two men stand in the street, saying nothing, enjoying a brief moment of silence. There is much to talk about, but none of it can be said, none of it is worth saying. After a while, Ismet puts his hand on Kenan's shoulder. "Good luck with your water. I'll call in on you tonight or maybe tomorrow." He digs his hands into his pockets and continues up the street.

Kenan watches him as he disappears around the corner, then picks up his water canisters and walks down the hill. His street runs into another, where there's a mirror that allows cars to see if anyone's coming. It's one of the few unbroken pieces of glass around, and every time Kenan passes it he's surprised to see it still undamaged. He finds it almost funny. There are hardly any cars on the roads, as those that aren't damaged beyond repair are inoperable due to the scarcity and resulting high price of fuel. What few moving cars there are have become the favorite targets of the men on the hills, and they're driven with a recklessness that makes them as dangerous as the city's attackers. The traffic lights don't work, the roads are full of holes and debris, and yet here's this mirror, without a scratch on it, working as well as it ever did.

He turns the corner, heading east before turning to the south again. He passes a building that has a soup kitchen in the basement and thinks that if they're open when he comes back he might see if he can get a meal. The supply of food in his kitchen is nearly exhausted, and if he can go without eating this evening it will mean more for the rest of the family.

A little further south he passes the Music Academy. The building is over a hundred years old, and has been training young musicians for forty. A harp sits atop a cupola facing the street corner. Between the windows of the third and the fourth floors, a rocket-propelled grenade has punched a hole through the wall. Inside, another grenade has blown through the wall in the main concert room, but still Kenan hears the sound of pianos coming from within. Several different pieces are being played in various parts of the building, and the music blends together, sometimes becoming unintelligible, a muddy noise of strings struck by hammers, but every so often one of the themes pauses, creating a space for another to emerge, and a few solitary notes of a melody slip out into the street.

After one quick block Kenan hits a main street. Before the war, he used to wait here for the tram that would take him three stops up the road to work. He's always liked the tram. To him, and others as well, the tram was one of the most tangible signs of civilization.

When the fighting began, Kenan was at work. Someone rushed into the room and announced that war had broken out. A few people started to panic, rushing to telephones, while others sat, stunned, not wanting to believe. Goran went to the window and looked out at the street. He came back smiling.

"There's no war. The trams are still running," he said, and sat back down at his desk. Kenan had also returned to work, along with several other colleagues. They didn't accept that the men on the hills could shoot at the trams, that their bullets would kill those inside. After all he's seen since then, the one sight he will never forget is that of a burning tram that had been hit first by a mortar and then by sniper fire, heaving thick inky smoke into the air. The trams haven't run since that day. They are scattered throughout the city, empty husks, some serving as cover against snipers, others simply left to rust. In Kenan's mind, whatever else happens, the war will not be over until the trams run again.

If he were to head west, two blocks to his right, he'd end

up at the marketplace. Without any food from the relief center, he's often forced to shop there at astronomically inflated prices. When the war began, one German mark, about half an American dollar, was worth ten Yugoslav dinar. Now, a mark costs a million dinar. Anyone who didn't convert their savings at the beginning of the war almost immediately became bankrupt. Not that it matters much. With prices nearly doubling each month, not many people had enough saved to last long anyway. Last month Kenan sold his family's washing machine on the black market for 110 marks. Without electricity it was useless to him. The last time he was at the market, a kilo of apples cost fifty marks, a kilo of potatoes twenty marks. Onions were twelve marks, beans eighteen, and for thirty marks you could get three packs of cigarettes. Sugar was sixty marks, coffee a hundred. Everything was easily twenty times more than it had cost before the war. Everything, that is, except incomes. Kenan doubts if he's made more than a thousand marks since the beginning of the war. He still has a few household items left to sell, but not many.

And yet some people seem untouched by financial pressures. They drive around in new Mercedeses, haven't lost any weight, and possess a ready supply of goods most people only remember from before the war. Kenan isn't sure how they do it, but he knows a lot of black-market food is being smuggled into Sarajevo through a tunnel that goes under the airport. To pass through it you need to know someone with pull in the government, and, although the tunnel is open twenty-four hours a day, hardly anyone gets through. Kenan suspects that what does go through is what is making the men in their sports cars rich. He can't understand how they can do it, how they can make money off trapped and starving people like him.

But there's little he can do about it. So he forgets about the marketplace, forgets about his empty stomach, and crosses the one-way street that encircles the main part of the old town. Here the terrain flattens out as the mountains give way to the bed of the valley. He has been coming here all his life. Every-where he looks reminds him of some memory, of something lost that can't be recovered. He wonders what will happen after, when the fighting stops. Even if each building is rebuilt so it's exactly as it was before, he doesn't know how he could sit in a comfortable chair and drink a coffee with a friend and not think about this war and all that went with it. But maybe, he thinks, he would like to try. He knows he doesn't want to give up the possibility.

Two different architects designed Strossmayer Street, one building the east side and the other the west. Kenan remembers coming here as a child with his parents, between Christmas and the New Year, to admire the way the street had been deco-rated. He was wearing a new coat and was very proud of how he looked in it. His mother called him handsome, and even his older sister, who teased him every chance she got, said it was a good coat. He held his father's hand as they walked down the street, stopping every once in a while to look at the lights, and his father spoke to him as though he were an adult. It's hard to see the street of his memory in the one he's on now.

If he continues south for another block he will come to the eastbound portion of the one-way street he crossed earlier. The main tram artery, it heads east until it comes to the National Library. It curves northward and then turns west, converging back on itself by the Vrbanja Bridge, across the river from Grbavica. If he were to keep going south, he'd cross the Miljacka River using the Ćumurija Bridge. At some point he'll have to cross the river to reach the brewery, but the Ćumurija is the least inviting bridge for him, even though it offers the shortest possible distance between his house and the opposite bank of the river. It has been shelled, and all that's left of it is its steel frame. He could still cross it by balancing on the skeleton of steel, but that is hard to do with the canisters, even when they're empty, and it would leave him an easy target for the men on the hills.

Keeping close to the buildings, Kenan turns east, opting instead to cross the river using the Princip Bridge. It's just as open to the hills to the south, but it's in much better shape, so he can cross it faster. He passes the remnants of the once grand Hotel Europa. There has been an inn on this site for over five hundred years. The last time it was destroyed, a little over a century ago, it was called the Stone Inn. A nearby merchant's storeroom caught fire, and the fire quickly reached the Stone

Inn, where there was a large army store of barrels of methyl alcohol. Some of the barrels exploded, and the fire spread west, engulfing much of the old town. Firefighters emptied the remaining barrels into the river, not taking into account that alcohol is lighter than water. When they put their pumps into the Miljacka the water they drew wasn't water at all but fire itself. By the time they realized their mistake it was too late, and much of the city was destroyed. Even now Kenan can see the demarcation of the street where they halted the Great Fire, where the old Turkish buildings end and the newer Austro-Hungarian ones begin.

What Kenan thinks about isn't the night of the fire, but the day after. What it must have looked like. Did it compare with what he sees today? But at least the Great Fire was over quickly. He doesn't know if today is the end or just the beginning. And he doesn't know what things will look like when and if it does end. How do you build it all up again? Do the people who destroyed the city also rebuild it? Is the city reconstructed so that it can be wiped away again someday, or do people believe that this will be the last time such a project will be necessary, that from now on things will last forever? Though he can't quite put his finger on the specifics of this question, he believes that the character of those who will build the city again is more important than the makeup of those who destroyed it. Of course the men on the hills are evil. There's no room for nuance in that. But if a city is made anew by men of questionable character, what will it be? He thinks of the men in the fancy cars who bought his washing machine with a few kilos of potatoes and onions. They shouldn't be the ones who get to make a new Sarajevo, if and when it is time for such a thing to be born.

He's almost at the Princip Bridge. It used to be called the Latin Bridge, but it's there that, in 1914, the First World War began. The footprints of the assassin Princip used to be marked on the place where he stood and killed the heir to the Hapsburg throne and his pregnant wife, but they're gone now, ruined or stolen. Archduke Franz Ferdinand's last words to his wife were, "Don't die, stay alive for our children." He wasn't supposed to be there, in that spot, but he had insisted on going to the hospital to check on the victims of an earlier attempt on his life. Princip had given up on his mission for the day and was eating a meal when he saw the archduke's car, stepped out onto the street, and fired two shots. As a schoolboy, Kenan had been made to visit the small museum, now destroyed, that commemorated the assassination. He has always been slightly ashamed that, for a generation, when the world thought of Sarajevo, it was as a place of murder. It isn't clear to him how the world will think of the city now that thousands have been murdered. He suspects that what the world wants most is not to think of it at all.

He's just about to turn south toward the bridge when a man comes running around the corner. Once safely behind the buildings he collapses, breathless. "Sniper," he says, pointing toward the bridge. "They're firing all along the left bank."

"I'm trying for the brewery," Kenan says, helping the man to his feet.

"You're best off crossing the Šeher Ćehaja."

Kenan pauses. The Šeher Ćehaja is the most eastern of the bridges crossing the Miljacka, and using it will require a significant detour, almost doubling the distance of his trip. As it is, he still has about a kilometer and a half to go before he reaches the brewery, and this route would add another two kilometers. "Are you sure?"

The man shrugs. "It's for you to say. Maybe he's not a very good shot. He missed me."

Any thoughts Kenan might have about risking a crossing are removed by the sound of a shell landing nearby, probably somewhere just across the river. There's a short burst of rifle fire, and then another shell lands. Kenan feels himself begin to panic, tries to take a few deep breaths. His mouth has gone dry.

"It's okay," the man says. "They can't get at us here." Kenan knows this isn't true, but the words do make him feel better, as does the knowledge that they aren't the target of the shelling. It seems to be moving farther away, or at least it isn't getting closer.

It's clear that he'll have to take the long way around, so he wishes the man luck and backtracks about fifty meters, heading north, just to be sure he's well away from the stretch where the men on the hills are shelling. He turns east when he hits the Sweet Corner, named after the cluster of pastry shops located here at the turn of the century, right on the dividing line between the eastern and western architecture of the old town.

As he enters the old Turkish neighborhood of Baščaršija, he feels as though he's returning to the scene of a crime. He hasn't been here since the day the library burned, and though he's still a distance from it, he can feel its proximity. For some reason the mess of shattered roof tiles and crumbled bricks in this part of town bothers him more than it does in other places. There are a few people in the streets, and down one narrow alley he sees a group of tin-men with small displays of items for sale. For months now they've been turning bullets and shell casings into pens, plates, anything they can sell. One man has built a small wood-burning stove, and even though he knows it's almost certainly more than he has, Kenan wonders how much he would sell it for.

Hardly anyone lives in Baščaršija. For half a millennium, it has served as the city's marketplace, its streets organized according to the type of trades conducted there. But in recent years this strict discipline had broken down a bit, with more and more shops selling merchandise designed for tourists. Now there are no more tourists, and the shops are closed just like everything else. To his north is the Sebilj, a gazebo-shaped public fountain that serves as a meeting place, or did. Its location, placed firmly in the middle of a large plaza, makes it an exceptionally poor place to be at present. Only pigeons are brave or stupid enough to congregate at its base.

As he passes the Sebilj, staying as close to the cover of buildings as possible, Kenan hears one of the pigeons squawk and sees the others flutter away. The pigeon skids toward him, seemingly moved by a gravity that pulls at it from the side. Kenan stops, confused, and watches as the pigeon disappears into the alcove of a doorway just ahead of him. The squawking halts abruptly, and after a few seconds a piece of bread flies out of the alcove. He looks closer and sees it's attached to something. Gradually the birds begin to return, and as one ventures closer to the bread he sees what's happening. Someone is fishing for pigeons.

He takes a few steps forward and looks into the alcove. There an old man holds a short fishing pole, his face intent on the plaza and his piece of bread. The man sees Kenan and waves slightly, not wanting him to disturb the line.

"How's the fishing today?" Kenan asks, trying to keep his voice low so as not to startle the birds.

"They're biting well," the man says, keeping his eyes on one gray bird who's eyeing the piece of bread.

"Do you need a license this time of year?" he asks, smiling so the man understands it's a joke.

The man looks at him, as if to discern whether he has some sort of official capacity. Eventually he smiles back. "Of course. You need a license for the fish, and also for the pole."

"Where do you get the license?"

The man points at the hills. "Up there you can get one. Just keep going up until you find the office."

The pigeon is close now. It seems to have its doubts, but another one is coming up behind it and its indecision is under pressure. It moves toward the bread.

"Is it expensive?" Kenan asks.

The man shakes his head. "No, but the lineup's very long. It could be quite a wait."

The gray pigeon hops ahead of its rival and lunges at the bread. It swallows it whole, and for a moment nothing happens. The pigeon appears pleased with itself. It has managed a small meal. Life is good. Then it's jerked hard from the inside, and it gives a sharp squawk as the man reels it in. The pigeon tries to fly away, but the man yanks in the line and pulls it back to earth.

"Sometimes they try to fly, sometimes they don't," he says. "I don't know what makes the difference."

He reels the struggling bird all the way in. When it's close enough, he reaches out and grabs it. For some reason it stops fighting him, perhaps in shock. The man holds the pigeon's body with one hand and, with the other, twists its neck until it breaks. Then he cuts the bird's body loose and places it in a bag beside him. The man stands.

"Are you finished for the day?" Kenan asks.

The old man nods. "I've caught six, one for each person in my apartment. I only take what I need. If I'm not greedy, perhaps they will still be here tomorrow."

"Good luck," Kenan says.

"To you too, sir." The man picks up his bag and pole and starts up the plaza, heading north toward Vratnik.

Kenan stays there long after the man is gone. Although he has never killed an animal himself, other than a fish, the idea of it never particularly bothered him. But he can't help feeling a sort of kinship with the pigeon. He thinks it's possible that the men on the hills are killing them slowly, a half-dozen at a time, so there will always be a few more to kill the next day.

arrow

The office of Arrow's unit commander isn't much to look at. A small room with a desk and three chairs, boarded-up windows, a stained carpet covering a badly worn wood floor. All of it is illuminated by one naked lightbulb powered by a generator that she can hear chugging away in another room. The bulb hangs from a wire into the middle of the room above the desk, and if she looks directly at it, she will be blinded for the following ten minutes by a glowing orb centered in her vision. She can never decide if the light has been placed in such an obtrusive location on purpose, as some sort of intimidation technique, or if it's only poor design. In her experience the army excels in both intimidation and tastelessness.

"You have been watched for some time now," her commander says, standing behind her and placing his hand on Arrow's shoulder in a way that seems as though it's meant to be reassuring. Arrow wonders whether he's referring to that morning's incident, to the enemy sniper who had been hunting her. In the time she spends considering this possibility, the hand on her shoulder goes from feeling benign to malevolent. She fights an urge to tear it off her, rise from the hard chair she sits in, and drive the palm of her hand upward into the throat of her unit commander.

"Many people are impressed with your abilities," he continues. It seems that he isn't talking about this morning's sniper, so she calms down. He removes his hand and sits behind his desk, facing her.

Nermin Filipović is a good-looking man, dressed in rumpled but clean camouflage fatigues. His beard is neatly trimmed and his hair is dark, if a little long. Arrow imagines it is soft to the touch. He's in his late thirties and, as far as she knows, isn't married. There's a small scar on his forehead above his right eye, and the nail on his right index finger has turned a dark purple, as though it has recently sustained a blow.

He's a professional soldier. When the war began, and Europe's fourth-largest army turned inward on itself and surrounded the city, he was one of the few career officers to break ranks and defend the city against his former colleagues. If they fail and Sarajevo falls, if the men on the hills ever make it into the city, he will be one of the first people they execute. Arrow isn't sure what her position will be on their list. There's no way to tell how much they know about her.

"We have a special assignment for you. An important assignment."

Arrow nods. She has suspected that he was working toward

something like this. So far they've been content to let her choose her own targets, have left her more or less alone, provided she continues to deliver bullets to worthy destinations. Lately, however, she has felt more attention being paid to her, and she knows that sooner or later they are going to ask her to do something she doesn't want to do.

"I would remind you of our first conversation," she says, looking him straight in the eye, something she rarely does.

Four months after the war started, Nermin had sent a man to request that she come see him. In a way, Arrow was surprised it had taken them so long to approach her. Most of the other members of the university target-shooting team had already been approached. She would learn later that her father, who was a policeman, had asked Nermin to leave her out of it. He was killed in one of the first battles of the war, in front of the Sarajevo Canton Building, and Arrow has never asked Nermin whether he felt her father would have changed his mind about her involvement in the city's defense or if he simply decided to ignore the request of a dead man. She doesn't want to know the answer.

"We need people who can shoot as well as you can," he said.

"I've never shot at a person," she replied, knowing that until quite recently this was probably true of most of the city's defenders, and maybe even its attackers. "Only at targets."

"It's a matter of perspective," he said.

"I don't want to kill people."

"You'd be saving lives. Every one of those men on the hills will kill some of us. Given the chance, they will kill all of us."

Arrow thought about this. She thought about what it might be like to pull the trigger and have her bullet hit a living being instead of a piece of paper. She was mildly surprised to find that the thought didn't horrify her, that she could probably do it, and that she could probably live with it.

"I think this will end," she said. Her hands turned her coffee cup in a clockwise circle. She hadn't drunk any of it yet, and soon it would be cold.

He leaned back in his chair and looked at the wall as if it were a window, as if it offered some view that could lend a new perspective to her statement. "That's a good view to take. I hope you're right. I don't see how it could last forever."

He turned his gaze back from the wall, seeming to sense that she was moving toward stating an intent.

Arrow nodded. "I think it will end, and when it does I want to be able to go back to the life I had before. I want my hands to be clean."

Nermin's eyes flickered down to where his own hands lay folded on his desk and then back up. She wasn't sure if he knew he had done this. It looked involuntary, but still it made her nervous. His hands moved to his lap. "I don't think any of us will be going back to the life we had before, however this ends. Even those who keep their hands clean."

"If I do this, it will have to be done a certain way. I won't blindly kill just because you say I must." She raised her cup to her mouth and drank. The coffee was good, strong and bitter, but no longer hot.

And so they reached an agreement. She would report only to Nermin, she would work alone, and she would, for the most part, choose her own targets. Occasionally Nermin has asked for someone specific, or that she work in a particular area, and thus far she has always been able to accommodate him.

She's aware, now, that the woman who sat in this office on that day and said she didn't want to kill anyone was gone, that with each passing week she's less and less certain there will be an end to all this. The parameters of their deal are dangerously close to irrelevance.

This does not, however, reduce her resolve. If anything, her desire to adhere to her conditions, to keep her hands clean, has increased. Although she has nearly completely lost sight of the person she was, she still knows who she wants to be, and as far as she can see, the only path leading her toward this person is back through her former self.

Nermin looks at her for a long time. She can see that he's considering saying something to her, and she suspects it's about her role in defending the city, but he doesn't. He stands, walks past her, and opens the door, motioning with his hand for her to follow him.

"I have something to show you," he says, turning to her. "Don't worry. This is as clean as you're going to get."

"Wait," Nermin says, looking at his watch. "It's almost time."

Arrow knows this street well. It's in the heart of the city, just past the point where Turkish buildings give way to Austro-Hungarian ones. Farther down is the Second World War memorial, the eternal flame, which has gone out. Behind her is a street where she used to meet friends for a coffee when she was in university, and the river isn't far to the south. And past that are the southern hills of the city, where a cable car once carried people to the top of Mount Trebević.

They're standing in the doorway of a shop that's no longer open, across from the indoor public market. Arrow knows that not long ago a mortar shell landed in this street and killed a large number of people. She heard all about it on the radio, but although it was unusual for so many to be killed in one spot at one time, she didn't think much about the incident then. It was simply how things were, she supposed. The opportunity to die was everywhere, and it just wasn't that surprising when that opportunity became an event. Now, however, standing in the street where it happened, it seems to her that something significant occurred here.

An explosion groans to the west of them, and Arrow involuntarily looks in the direction of the sound.

Nermin, who hasn't looked, smiles. "I think they're trying to send us a message."

"What is the message?" she asks as another shell lands in the same area.

Nermin shrugs. "I don't know. I'm making a special effort not to listen. Okay, here he comes."

At first, Arrow isn't sure whether to trust what she sees. She even wonders if it's possible she's hallucinating, or if perhaps she has died and this is how the transition to whatever follows death takes place, through a series of unbelievable circumstances. But gradually she accepts she's still alive, and she's lucid, and this is happening.

A tall man with turbulent black hair, an almost comic mustache, and the saddest face she has ever seen emerges from a doorway. He wears a slightly dusty tuxedo and carries a cello under one arm, a stool under the other. He walks out of the building with a calm and determined stride, appearing oblivious to the danger he's putting himself in, sets his stool in the middle of the street, sits down, and places his instrument between his legs.

"What is he doing?" she asks, but Nermin doesn't answer.

The cellist closes his eyes and remains still, his arms hanging limp. It appears as though the cello stays upright of its own will, independent of the man surrounding it. The wood glows rich and warm against the drab gray of shattered paving stones, and she feels an urge to touch it, to run her fingers over the lacquered surface. Her hand reaches out, a futile attempt to bridge a distance far greater than the thirty or so meters that separate her from the cello.

The cellist opens his eyes. The sadness she saw in his face is gone. She doesn't know where it went. His arms rise, and his left hand grips the neck of the cello, his right guides the bow to its throat. It is the most beautiful thing she has ever seen. When the first notes sound they are, to her, inaudible. Sound has vanished from the world.

She leans back into the wall. She's no longer there. Her mother is lifting her up, spinning her around and laughing. The warm tongue of a dog licks her arm. There's a rush of air as a snowball flies past her face. She slips on someone else's blood and lands on her side, a severed arm almost touching her nose. In a movie theater, a boy she likes kisses her and puts his hand on her stomach. She exhales, and pulls the trigger.

Then sound returns to the world. She isn't sure what has happened. She doesn't know what a man playing a cello in the street at four in the afternoon has done to her. You will not cry, she tells herself, and she wills herself calm until after the cellist has finished, risen, and returned to the building he came from. There will be no crack in her.

Nermin is looking at her.

"We need you to keep this man alive," he says.

"I don't understand." She's barely heard what he said and struggles to bring herself back into her situation.

Nermin removes his hat and wipes his sleeve across his

brow. "He has said that he will do this for twenty-two days. This is the eighth. People see him. The world has seen him. We cannot allow him to be killed."

"I can't be responsible for him," she says. She's tired. She's almost always tired, but she can't remember the last time she acknowledged it, even to herself. An old woman shuffles past them, keeping close to the wall, and Arrow wonders which one of them is more exhausted.

Nermin shakes his head. "I'm not asking that of you. We require something slightly different."

The place where the cellist sits, while vulnerable to shells, he says, isn't within the direct line of fire for a sniper on the southern hills. But they have received information. It's believed that the enemy will send a sniper into their part of the city to shoot him. And her job will be to stop that. It is, they admit, almost impossible. But, as Nermin reminds her, she has a certain talent for the impossible.

"Why don't they just shell the street again?"

"It's not about merely killing him. Shooting him is a statement."

Arrow leans back against the wall and pictures the cellist lying in the street. She sees Nermin's point. A bullet leaves evidence that a mortar doesn't.

"Look," he says, "we have made you a deal, and I will continue to do my best to honor it. But things are changing on our side. If you can do this, we would both benefit."

"I don't kill to benefit myself, or you."

"I know. I'm just not sure how much longer that will be a position you or I can afford to take." Nermin leans in, kisses her on each cheek, then turns and walks away. For a while she stands, not moving, not thinking. She just wants things to be still. But then the shelling begins again, and so she forces her feet to move, pulls her coat tight around her shoulders, and heads for home.

dragan

It's possible the sniper is gone. At least ten minutes have passed since he fired, and already several people have made it through the intersection without incident. Dragan moves closer to the edge of the street, contemplating crossing. He's hungry, feels the emptiness of his stomach urge him across. The bakery is on the other side. Only two more especially dangerous crossings and he will have bread. But another part of him knows there's no hurry. He's not going to starve to death over a few extra minutes of waiting, whereas a lack of caution will get him killed quicker than anything.

He steps back a bit, turns to lean against the warm metal of the railcar shielding him from Grbavica and the hills above, up to Vraca, the old war fort. He used to take his wife and son to Vraca for picnics in the summer, when they didn't have time to go to the park at Ilidža or up Mount Trebević. From there you could see most of the city, a fact that has taken on a whole new significance in recent months.

To his right a woman approaches, and as she gets closer

Dragan recognizes her. Her name is Emina. She's a friend of his wife, about fifteen years younger than he. Dragan has always liked her, but he doesn't much care for her husband, Jovan. Whenever they went out for supper, which they did regularly before the war, Dragan was stuck talking to Jovan, whose only apparent interest was politics, a subject Dragan has no patience for. After a while, he began to make excuses to get out of these dinners, until, shortly before the fighting broke out, the invitations stopped and his wife and Emina drifted out of contact.

It's obvious to Dragan that Emina has seen him, is coming to speak to him, and he looks for somewhere to hide even though it's pointless. There's no way to prevent this interaction, short of running into the street, and although Dragan can barely bring himself to nod a polite hello to a stranger, let alone talk to an old friend, he isn't yet willing to risk his life to avoid a social exchange. This comforts him slightly, but he wonders if it's possible that a day will come when he makes a different choice.

Hoping for a miracle, he stares down at his feet, attempting to appear deep in thought. Perhaps she will walk by him. It's not impossible. It could be that she'll walk right by him without seeing him and continue into the street, arriving safely on the other side without even knowing he was there. What he wants is to cross and get his loaf of bread as quickly as he can. He doesn't want to encounter anyone.

"Dragan, is that you?" A hand touches his shoulder, and he realizes that his attempt to look as though he was deep in thought resulted in actual thinking. He smiles, finding this funny, and Emina smiles back.

"Hello, Emina," he says, leaning in to kiss her on each cheek. She hugs him tight. She feels small beneath her blue wool coat. He remembers this coat. His wife once told him that she liked it, and he'd always meant to ask Emina where she got it, so he could buy one for Raza, but he never did.

"How are you? How is Raza? Where are you staying?"

He tells her as much as he can, tells her about how his wife and son left on one of the last buses out of Sarajevo, how their apartment was one of the first shelled, and how he's staying with his sister. He can't tell her about how his wife and son left at night and when the bus pulled away he felt, somehow, that he would never see them again, even though they were going to be only a few hundred kilometers away, not even an hour by plane. He can't tell her about the night his apartment was shelled, how he hid in the cellar with his neighbors and waited for the building to come down on top of them, or how he arrived the next day at his sister's, his brother-in-law answering the door and looking at him as if it were his fault his apartment was destroyed. He thinks that if he were to tell her all the things he can't tell anyone, they would be standing there for days.

She looks at him, and he can see she knows there's more to his story than he's telling her, but she doesn't push him. Everyone has more than they declare. He isn't sure what to say next.

Should he ask about Jovan? What if something's happened to him, or what if he's left her? At the very least she'll be reminded that Dragan never really liked him, and that in itself will be awkward enough.

Emina isn't moving, she's just standing there, waiting for him to speak. Her hair is tied back, but a few brown strands have fallen across her face. She brushes them aside, tucking them behind her ear, and puts her hand back in her coat pocket. She seems smaller than Dragan remembered, not just thinner but shorter. He's not sure how that is possible.

If only to break this awkward silence, he speaks. "How is Jovan?" he asks, afraid of the answer.

She shrugs. "He joined the army. I don't see much of him."

Dragan is surprised. Jovan didn't strike him as the sort. He'd always pegged him as more of a talker than a fighter.

Emina hesitates, perhaps seeing his surprise. "Well, he's more of a liaison for the government between the various branches of the army." This makes much more sense. "I'm not really sure exactly what it is he does. All I know is that he's gone almost all the time."

Dragan nods, not sure what to say. "There's a sniper covering this intersection. Or at least there was a few minutes ago. I'm waiting to see if he's gone."

"Did he get anyone?" Emina looks genuinely concerned. This strikes Dragan as odd. He isn't indifferent to the deaths around him, but he can't really say that he feels them so much that they would register on his face. He doesn't think many other people do either, anymore.

"No," he says. "He doesn't look to be a very good shot."

She appears to think about this. He hopes she doesn't take it too seriously. He doesn't know how good a shot the sniper is. All he knows is that he missed the last time he shot. There's no way to tell how many other times he's fired without missing.

"I think I'll wait a bit. I'm not in any real hurry," she says. She tells him she's on her way to deliver some medicine to a woman a few blocks southwest of the bakery. Radio Sarajevo has organized a medical swap, where people who have old prescriptions they aren't using can give them to those who need various drugs that are no longer available. Each day they read out who needs what over the radio, and those who can help do. The woman she's going to see has a heart condition and uses the same medication as Emina's mother, who died about five years ago. Although the drugs are beyond their use-by date, they're still better than nothing. "After all," she says, "they're just blood thinners. I don't think they really expire."

"No," Dragan says. "You're probably right."

"It's the same stuff as rat poison, and that doesn't expire."

"It is?"

"Well, there's a little arsenic in it. Or I think there is. My mother used to joke about it."

Dragan had met Emina's mother once, a year before she died. She looked a lot like Emina, but her sense of humor ran darker than her daughter's. It was apparent she didn't think much of Jovan either. When he tried to steer the discussion toward politics, as he always did, she threw her hands up in the air. "You and your politics. Nothing good will happen because of politics."

"Nothing good will happen without politics," Jovan replied, shaking his head.

"Which one of them," Emina said, "do you suppose is the optimist in the family?"

Dragan and his wife laughed, but the question perplexed him, and he wasn't sure that Emina was joking.

"Do you know the difference between an optimist and a pessimist?" Emina's mother asked, looking at Jovan, who appeared to have heard this before. A small hint of a smile cracked his lips. "A pessimist says, 'Oh dear, things can't possibly get any worse.' And an optimist says, 'Don't be so sad. Things can always get worse.'"

When she died, Dragan didn't go to the funeral. He can't remember why now. It's possible he wasn't invited, but more likely he was and had made some excuse not to go.

"Do you remember Ismira Sidran?" Emina asks him.

He does. She was the director of a theater company. They had done a production of *Hair* some years ago that was a big success. Dragan has seen several of her shows since then. She was a friend of Emina's, and once he met her on the street, walking with Emina. She struck him as a loud, difficult woman, and he'd been irritated by her.

"This year is the twenty-five-year anniversary of the first performance of *Hair* on Broadway, and she was invited to bring her company to New York for a performance or a celebration or something." The sun has come out from behind a cloud, and it's warming up fast. Emina unclasps the top button on her coat.

"Did the government approve it?" Dragan is surprised. They've been very selective about who they let leave the city.

"Sure, to start with. I saw her, and she told me there were thirty-two people on the list. 'Thirty-two!' I said. 'That's so many people.' But she said that it took that many to run the lights and the props and all that stuff, people you never see from the audience. So that seemed okay. But then I saw her a week or two later, and the list had another thirty names on it, and she said it still wasn't complete."

Dragan shakes his head. "It couldn't possibly take that many people."

"No, but that's not the worst of it." Emina undoes another button on her coat. "By the time the list was submitted, there were nearly two hundred people on it."

"Did they let them go?"

"No. They knew they wouldn't come back."

It never used to be like this. Before the war, even when the country was a Communist state, you could travel anywhere you wanted. There were only four countries in the world that you needed a visa to visit. Now, though, no one leaves without permission. "They should have kept it to just the first thirty-two," Dragan says. "Then they could have got out."

"Jovan says it wouldn't have mattered. He says they would never have let any of them go."

"Maybe. But maybe some of them could have gone. Just a few. Maybe they could have escaped all this."

Emina looks up at the sky. "There's no way to tell."

"I would go if I could, I think." He knows this is a dangerous thing to say. People resent those who manage to get out. They're considered cowards, and although he suspects that anyone who's still sane would wish to leave, very few people will admit it, even to themselves, and fewer still would ever say so out loud.

There are only two ways out now. Either you know someone with power and you get a pass through the tunnel, or you have money. Other than that, you're stuck. Those who had power or money when the war began have mostly already left, and those who have power or money now have it because of the war, so have no incentive to leave.

Emina doesn't appear shocked by his admission, though. "Why didn't you leave with Raza?"

He shrugs. "I didn't think that it would go on for this long. I wanted to protect our apartment, and I didn't want to lose my job. Maybe I made a mistake."

"No. We have to stay. If we all go they will come down from the hills and the city will be theirs."

"If we stay they will shoot at us from the hills until we're all dead, and then they'll come down just the same."

"The world will never allow that. They'll have to help us sooner or later," she says. He's not sure from her tone of voice if she believes what she says. He doesn't know how she could. They must both see the same city disintegrating around them.

"No one is coming." His voice is harsher than he means it to be. "We're here on our own, and no one's coming to help us. Don't you know that?"

Emina looks down, and fastens the top two buttons on her coat. She puts her hands in her pockets. After a while she says, very quietly, "I know no one is coming. I just don't want to believe it."

Dragan knows exactly what she means. He doesn't want to believe it either. For a long time he held out hope, listened to the news, waited for someone to put a stop to this madness. All his life he has lived under the rule of law. If you broke the law, the police would arrest you. There was order, and it was un-questioned. Then, in the blink of an eye, it all fell apart. Like many others, Dragan waited far longer for order to be restored than was logical. He tried to go about his life as though things were still normal, as though someone was in charge. The men on the hills were a minor inconvenience that would be resolved at any moment. Sanity would prevail. But then, one day, he could no longer fool himself. This wasn't a temporary situation, a momentary glitch in the system, and no one was going to fix it.

"I worked at the bakery with a man who survived Jasenovac, and then Auschwitz," Dragan says. The man had retired five or six years before there were men on the hills, but Dragan had still seen him every so often. They would meet for a coffee, or occasionally a glass of plum brandy. He had never spoken to Dragan of his life during the war until one day shortly before the fighting began, when he told him about being in the camps. He told him how at Jasenovac the guards had a competition to see who could kill the most people in one day. The winner, a guard named Petar Brzica, killed 1,360 people with a butcher's knife. For winning this contest he was given some wine, a suckling pig, and a gold watch. After the war he escaped to the United States, where his name is on a list of resident war criminals to this day. Many of those killed were the fathers and grandfathers of the men on the hills, and of the people they are shooting at.

"The last time I saw him, he told me, 'What is coming is worse than anything you can imagine,'" Dragan says. "He killed himself the day the war began."

Emina shakes her head. "This cannot be as bad as what happened in those camps."

Dragan considers this, wonders how relative suffering is.

"No, it's not. I don't think he thought it would be. But I think he believed that what he and others suffered there meant something, that people had learned from it. But they haven't."

"Haven't they?" Emina asks.

"Look around," Dragan answers.

Though he'd intended it as a rhetorical statement, Emina does indeed look around. Prompted by her, Dragan does too, and he wonders if she sees the same things he sees. Does she see the gray that is everywhere? Does she see the mangled buildings, the wreckage in the streets, the people grown thin and tired, slinking along like frightened animals? She must. How could she not?

He doesn't know why she sought him out, why she didn't just walk by him and pretend he wasn't there. There was no need for this. He didn't need to see how much the war had taken from her, or from him.

"One of the things about the war," she says, "is that I've been down a lot of streets I'd never been on before. It has changed my geography."

Dragan nods. He has noticed the same thing, found it curious to learn how much of the city he's lived in his whole life was a block or two outside his experience, how a shell here and a sniper there have altered which streets are familiar and which are only vaguely known.

"There's a street near my house that, before the war, I never walked down," Emina continues. "But with the sniper at the bottom of the street I had to go the long way around, so I found myself in this new street.

"There was a house there with a huge cherry tree in the yard, full of ripe fruit. An old woman was picking the cherries. She must have had fifteen or twenty kilograms of fruit picked, and there was still more on the tree.

"I went up to her, mostly because I had never seen a tree like that in Sarajevo, had no idea these cherries grew here.

"'That's a beautiful tree,' I said to her, and she told me her mother had planted it when she was a girl, and that it had always given good fruit. She was picking the fruit for her grandchildren, but was a little worried, because you can't give children only sweet things. I suggested she sell some of the cherries, and she told me that perhaps she would.

"By coincidence, a few days later Jovan brought home some salt he'd got from someone, a huge five-kilogram bag. It was far more than we needed or could ever use. I thought of the woman, and when I went by I took her a kilogram."

Emina's face is relaxed, and her voice is soft. Dragan isn't really sure what the point of her story is, but he's happy that she is telling him.

"The woman was beside herself. I've never seen anyone smile so much. She actually hugged me. Over a kilogram of salt. As I was leaving, she gave me two big pails full of cherries. A ridiculous amount. I said, 'I can't possibly eat all these. I don't have any children, it's just me and my husband.' But she insisted. 'Give them away,' she said. 'Do whatever you like with them. I have more than I need.' So I gave them to our neighbors, a small basket to ten different families."

"You were good to give her the salt," Dragan says, and he means it.

"I didn't need it. She didn't have to give me the cherries, either." Emina shrugs. "Isn't that how we're supposed to behave? Isn't that how we used to be?"

"I don't know," Dragan says. "I can't remember if we were like that, or just think we were. It seems impossible to remember what things were like." And he suspects this is what the men on the hills want most. They would, of course, like to kill them all, but if they can't, they would like to make them forget how they used to be, how civilized people act. He wonders how long it will take before they succeed.

As long as he stands here waiting to cross, he knows, they're winning. It's time his day, his life, moved through this intersection and toward whatever end awaits him.

"I think I'll cross now," he says to Emina.

"Okay," she says. "I'll follow after you."

Dragan moves toward the intersection. His stomach hurts. When he's one step away from being out in the open he takes a deep breath and runs. He tries to keep his head low, but after three steps he feels his back begin to ache and he straightens up. His lungs are raw, his legs like rubber. He can't believe he isn't yet even a quarter of the way across. He has never felt so old.

He feels the shot an instant before he hears it. There is a sharp zip, a rush of air as a bullet snaps past his left ear, then the harsh blast of a gun. For an instant he wonders if he's been shot. He knows that he'd be dead if he was. He heard the bullet, and that means the sniper missed. He's surprised, confused, and frightened. It's not clear to him what he should do. For no more than two seconds he stands motionless, frozen. It seems like millennia.

Then he runs, back the way he came. He doesn't feel his lungs or his legs or his stomach. He becomes automatic, an animal, and he flees. His body is braced for the sniper's next shot, the one that will finish him. The closer he gets to safety, the more he expects it. He can see Emina standing behind the boxcar. Her mouth hangs open, her face contorted, and he thinks he hears her calling his name.

His shoulder slams into metal, and his legs give out. Emina grabs his arm as he tries not to fall, and the world around him blurs. People are asking him if he's okay, and he thinks he is, but he can't answer them. This is the first time Dragan has ever been shot at. He's been in places where there has been shooting, and he's been in areas where shells have fallen, but no one has ever marked him specifically for death before. A part of him can't believe it's happened, and a part can't believe he's survived.

Slowly he recovers his senses. He's still out of breath, panting like a dog, but he finds himself able to speak. When Emina asks him, for at least the tenth time, "Are you hurt?" he's able to answer her.

"I told you he wasn't a very good shot," he says.

Emina looks at him, unsure. Something in him, he wishes he knew what, seems to reassure her. Her face relaxes, and her hand rubs his back. "Sarajevo roulette," she says. "So much more complicated than Russian."

He laughs, not because it's funny but because it's true, and he stands there, Emina's hand on his back, glad for the first time in a long while to be alive.

arrow

She dresses in silence, picks up her rifle, and closes the door to the apartment. Her footsteps echo in the stairwell despite her efforts at stealth. It's a quirk of the building's design, she supposes, and considers whether an inability to muffle sound would be described as a positive or a negative acoustic quality. She decides it all depends on what you want out of a staircase. There are advantages to being able to hear who's in the hallway.

The sun has been up for half an hour, but the streets are mostly deserted. She encounters a few people as she moves down the hill and into the old town, but she doesn't make eye contact with them. She passes the remnants of a shop that once sold the best ice cream, and she remembers being a small girl with her grandmother on this street. She asked her grandmother to stop, in the pleading voice of a child used to getting her way, even though she'd just had some ice cream not an hour earlier. When her grandmother said no, Arrow let go of her hand and refused to continue. Her grandmother knelt down, took Arrow's face in her hands, and kissed her on the forehead.

"There is more to life than ice cream," she said.

Arrow wonders, as this memory fades, what she would give up for a scoop of that ice cream today. All the money she has? Certainly. Her rifle? Maybe. The one remaining photograph of her grandmother? She shakes her head and increases her pace, denying her mind a chance to answer.

This is her favorite time of day. It's nearly always quiet. Even the war stops for a rest, if only a short one. The absence of shelling is almost like music, and she imagines if she closed her eyes she could convince herself that she was walking through the streets of Sarajevo as it used to be. Almost. She knows that in the city of her memory she wasn't hungry, and she wasn't bruised, and her shoulder didn't bear the weight of a gun. In the city of her memory there were always people out at this time of morning, preparing for the day to come. They wouldn't be shut inside like invalids, exhausted from another night of wondering if a shell was about to land on their house.

She has arrived at her destination. She stands where she stood the day before, her back against the same wall, and takes in the street. Paving stones that withstood the feet of generations have been split open. There's no glass left in the windows. Some of them are black-eyed, covered in plastic, while others are empty, gaps like absent teeth in an old man's mouth. The street has been assaulted.

Arrow crosses and sits in the spot where the mortar landed, the spot where, later today, the cellist will sit. She knows that twenty-two people died here and a multitude were injured, will not walk or see or touch again. Because they tried to buy bread. A small decision. Nothing to think about. You're hungry, and come to this place where maybe they will have some bread to buy. Of all the places to go, you come here. Of all the days to come, a particular one chooses you. At four o'clock in the afternoon. It's just something you do because life is a series of tiny, unavoidable decisions. And then some men on the hills send a bomb through the air to kill you. For them, it was probably just one more bomb in a day of many. Not notable at all.

She reaches down and picks up a small piece of glass. Glass is disappearing from the city. It's either blown up or removed to prevent it from becoming a lethal projectile when it inevitably is blown up. One pane at a time the windows through which people see the world are vanishing.

This is how she now believes life happens. One small thing at a time. A series of inconsequential junctions, any or none of which can lead to salvation or disaster. There are no grand moments where a person does or does not perform the act that defines their humanity. There are only moments that appear, briefly, to be this way.

She thinks of this in the context of pulling the trigger and ending a life. Before she ever killed, she had assumed this would put her life at a clear crossroads. She would behave in a way that demarcated the sort of person she had become. She expected to feel altered somehow from the person she was, or hoped to be. But that wasn't the case. It was the easiest thing in the world to pull the trigger, a nonevent. Everything that came before, all the small things that somehow added up without her ever noticing, made the act of killing an afterthought. This is what makes her a weapon. A weapon does not decide whether or not to kill. A weapon is a manifestation of a decision that has already been made.

The cellist confuses her. She doesn't know what he hopes to achieve with his playing. He can't believe he will stop the war. He can't believe he will save lives. Perhaps he has gone insane, but she doesn't think so. She's seen the faces of those who have cracked, seen them walk into the street without a care for the danger. She's seen them die, or survive, and to them it doesn't appear to register as different. The cellist doesn't strike her as a man who has lost his will to live. He appears to care about the quality of his life. She can't tell what he believes, and it bothers her that she can't say exactly what it is, or whether she wants to believe it too. She knows it involves motion. Whatever the cellist is doing, he isn't sitting in a street waiting for something to happen. He is, it seems to her, increasing the speed of things. Whatever happens will come sooner because of him.

She drops the piece of glass she has been turning over in her hand, listens to the small tick it makes as it returns to the ground. She wonders what will become of it. How long will it sit in the road? Will it be ground into dust that blows away or mixes in with the world, attached to someone's shoe, the tire of a car, the wing of a pigeon, the moisture in the atmosphere? Arrow wonders if the piece of glass will still be here tomorrow, and if, in any larger sense, she's very different from a piece of incidental detritus lying forgotten at the scene of a massacre.

Arrow will keep this man alive. This wasn't ever really in doubt, but neither had she decided she would do it. Now, as she sits where he sits, she tells herself that she will not allow this man to die. He will finish what he's doing. It isn't important whether she understands what he's doing or why he's doing it. She does understand it's important, and that is enough.

Her attention shifts toward the surrounding buildings. There are a lot of possible locations for someone wanting to shoot at this spot, but they all fall into two lines of fire, east to west or west to east. The buildings on either side of the street, while providing many hiding spots, also shield the cellist from the hills to the north and south. So they can't shoot from their own territory. They'll have to enter hers. And she presumes that they will wish to escape when they are finished. This narrows their possibilities. She decides that the most logical route of escape is to the south, across the river, into Grbavica. A shot from the southwest side of the street would therefore make the most sense.

But Arrow knows they won't send an ordinary man. Most of their snipers are either hired mercenaries or untrained soldiers. A mercenary would be unlikely to accept such a dangerous job. They prefer to sit on the hills and earn their dirty money in relative safety. An irregular soldier, however, wouldn't possess the skills necessary to pull this off and still escape, so unless a commander were sending a man on a suicide mission, it won't be an ordinary soldier she's facing. No, the person they send will be a properly trained army sniper, and he'll know what he's doing.

He won't be in the southwest, because he'll know that as soon as the cellist falls, every defender in the area will try to cut off access to Grbavica. It's simple geography. So the sniper will head in the opposite direction, and either try to slip into the hills to the north or hole up in a safe house until he can move. Either way, he will not go to the southwest.

Arrow looks to the east, and right away she sees where he will be. Not the exact building, but if he's any good, if he thinks in terms of a bullet's path and his need to escape, there's really only one area from which he can make a shot.

She stands and begins to walk east, toward where the shot will come from. She needs to find a spot from where she can target the sniper, but not be in either his natural sight line or an obvious position for a countersniper. He will anticipate her presence, and before he even begins to think about killing the cellist, he'll seek to assure himself that he's safe. He'll look for the best place for her to kill him from. Should she be detected, his first shot will be at her, his second at the cellist. That, at least, is what Arrow would do.

Directly above the cellist's position is the exact sort of

location that someone who didn't really know what they were doing would pick. An apartment building that affords a clear view of the street and the spot from which most would assume a countersniper would fire. If she were going to kill the cellist, she would turn her scope to this building with the full expectation of finding a rifle waiting for her here.

Arrow smiles. A plan is beginning to crystallize in her mind. She backtracks up the street, to the west, and selects a building on the south side that affords her a view of the area where she knows her enemy will be. She then walks back to where the cellist will play and sits, confirming the logistics of what she has mapped out. She wonders if the cellist is aware that someone's protecting him, and if he is, whether this knowledge brings him comfort. The street is still empty, and the air is cool. Soon the sun will begin to warm the ground and more people will venture out. At four o'clock some of these people might lean against a wall on the southern side of the street and watch the cellist play for a few minutes before continuing on their way. They will be unaware of what goes on above them until she fires, and even then it will be just one more gunshot in a day of hundreds.

Hours later, Arrow crouches in a room on the south side of the street, to the west of the place where soon the cellist will play. She's a few buildings past where an untalented sniper would shoot the cellist from. She has cut two holes in the plastic covering the window. One affords her a view of where she believes the enemy sniper will set up, to the northeast of her, and the other offers her access to the area where he will think she is, above the cellist. It's a perfect spot. There's no need for her to extend the barrel of her rifle into the street to make a shot, reducing the chances of her opposition spotting her. He'll be at a disadvantage to begin with, as the sun will be heading westward, which won't interfere with his shot at the cellist but will make it difficult for him to see Arrow's position.

Every factor is in Arrow's favor save one. If she has made a mistake, if they haven't sent a sniper who knows what he's doing, and he sets up on the southwest side of the street, she'll have no shot at him. She doesn't think she's made a mistake, but of course there's no way to tell for sure. It's another tiny gamble of life, she supposes, though a part of her wonders how tiny this particular one is.

On the third floor of a building on the north side of the street, above where the cellist will play, she has set a trap. In a window of an abandoned apartment she has placed a rifle, its barrel pointing west, toward where a sniper would place himself. The barrel of the rifle extends slightly through a hole in the window's plastic and, from the building where she thinks the sniper will be, the shadowy outline of a baseball cap is visible. If the sniper does what almost all snipers would do, what Arrow herself would do, he will fire at the hat before firing at the cellist. Often there wouldn't be time to do this, but a man sitting in the street playing a cello will not be able to move quickly, and he will still be there to shoot a few seconds later. So it would be best to eliminate first the person most likely to shoot you in return. And when the sniper fires at her decoy, if Arrow hasn't already spotted him, he'll give his position away. It's a crude trick, she knows, but because the sun will be in his eyes, and because the plastic covering the window will not allow him a clear view of the inside of the apartment, and because it will be too early in the day to use a night-vision scope, which she herself does not possess, the sniper won't perceive this trap. An exceptional sniper might notice that his secondary target never moved or be put off by the obviousness of the situation, but she's banking that her adversary is simply good and not unusually talented.

The glitch in her plan is that she isn't completely sure the apartment where she has placed her bait is deserted. It appears as though no one lives there, but nearly every building in the city contains seemingly uninhabitable apartments that are, in fact, lived in. If someone were to return, she would be in a predicament. Their presence wouldn't go unnoticed by the enemy sniper, and he'd more than likely assume they were soldiers. Not that this makes much of a difference. The enemy's snipers don't take into account who's a soldier and who isn't. But, given a choice, Arrow believes they would kill a soldier first.

It's a simple matter of survival. She doesn't want this blood on her hands, someone whose only mistake was coming home early. Though it happens every day, many times each day, it has never been Arrow's fault, and she intends that it never will be. She will not be responsible for the death of people who do not deserve to die.

This is why there are two holes in the plastic of her window. She has decided that, at any time, should she detect movement in the apartment above the cellist, she will fire. She won't hit anything, but the incoming fire will cause whoever is inside to seek cover, taking them out of the enemy sniper's sights. She'll then send a bullet in the sniper's general direction, to let him know that she knows where he is. If he's like most, that will be enough to convince him to rethink his plans for the day and flee. He'll come back, she knows, but she'll deal with that when it happens.

At least she's confident about the apartment she's in. A discreet conversation with the man guarding its entrance confirmed that its inhabitants had left, and two packs of cigarettes were enough to convince him to allow her inside and keep her whereabouts to himself. It's common for the residents of individual buildings to form a security watch among themselves, set in shifts, to keep snipers and other unwanted parties out, but it's a simple matter to evade these people if you know what you're doing. A bored man is easily distracted, and a frightened man is distracted to begin with. Slipping undetected into a guarded building is child's work. Arrow has done so more times than she can count.

The apartment she's in was once a nice home. Its windows are large and its rooms spacious. It's relatively intact, though a shell has hit the bathroom and reduced the sink, tub, and toilet to a pile of rubble. On the walls opposite the window daggers of glass stick out of the plaster like darts stuck in a corkboard, and a slush of human occupation, papers, photographs, a shredded sofa, lies discarded. Someone will come along eventually to pick it all up, if only to burn as fuel. She tries not to wonder too much about the people who used to live here, what they were like, if they were happy, if they are still alive, if they died here.

Through her scope she scans the buildings to the east. If the sniper is coming, he will already be in place. Over the last few hours she has been watching the street, noting which apartments have legitimate-looking people in them, which have people in them who bear watching, and, particularly, which windows show nothing. But most of all she has been establishing a base appreciation for how things are, so that when anything changes she'll know it. Out of the corner of her eye she keeps a constant vigil on the decoy apartment. She has so far detected no movement from within.

There are, in particular, three windows that give her pause. They're situated in excellent positions from which to fire on the street below, and each is located close to a stairwell, affording an escape route that's unlikely to be impeded. There has been no activity she can see, which is exactly how it would be were there a sniper inside.

She's growing confident in her plan, despite the fact that she still doesn't know where the sniper is. This conviction isn't based on anything rational. She hasn't obtained even one piece of information eliminating the possibility that he's somewhere in her area, to the west of the cellist, waiting for him to emerge. He could, for all she knows, be in the apartment beside her, below her, or on the roof above her. If he's a fool he will have saved himself. But with each passing minute she feels more certain he isn't a fool. She knows he is in one of the three windows.

Though she isn't looking, Arrow is immediately aware that the cellist has stepped out of his doorway. Before he has unfolded his stool and set it down in the middle of the street she has scanned the three windows a half-dozen times, and has completed two sweeps of the general area. As he closes his eyes and lowers his arms to hang at his side she glances down at him, only for a second, and then while he sits motionless she checks the windows four more times. She sees nothing.

A shell explodes in a distant sector of the city, and for an instant she thinks she sees something in one of the windows. It's on the fourth floor of an apartment building about seventy meters east of the cellist. She can't tell what it is. A shadow perhaps, some slight, nearly indiscernible movement. She's not sure it's anything at all.

As she checks the other two possibilities she can't shake the feeling that each time she looks away from the fourth-floor window she's missing something. Calm down, she tells herself. Let this come to you. Let things happen as they are going to happen, and react as you are going to react. Don't complicate it.

She takes an overview of the eastern section of the street, both the north and south sides. She searches for any small detail that might have changed, a moved brick, a change in a shadow. She tries not to get caught up in wondering if there's a difference or not. If there is, she will know. If there isn't, thinking about it isn't going to make it so. The temptation to second-guess is great, but she doesn't succumb.

The cellist lifts his bow and begins to play. The sound drifts up to Arrow, sometimes nearly inaudible, sometimes so clear and loud it seems he's in the room. Three floors above him, her decoy sits undisturbed. The apartment remains empty. Her trap, so far, has not succeeded, but nor has it failed.

The fourth-floor window draws her back to it. On first glance she almost misses what's changed. She's just about to move her attention to one of the other windows when she sees a hole in the plastic, perhaps three centimeters long, on the lower right-hand side. It's not big enough to aim and fire through, but it's large enough to see through. This would be his first step.

She considers taking a chance. She could send a bullet through that hole. If he's looking through it he will be killed, or at least severely injured. But if he isn't, he'll escape, and she'll be back to square one. Also, she reminds herself, she has no way of knowing who's in the apartment. She can't go firing bullets into apartments without being sure of who's inside, though she knows she's right. She knows he's inside.

There's movement in her peripheral vision. She looks down to the street. Two girls, not quite teenagers, have approached the cellist and are a few feet away from him. They stand, thin and serious, and they listen to him play. If he knows they're there he gives no indication. They're directly in the sniper's line of fire.

Arrow snaps back to the fourth-floor window. The hole in the plastic hasn't grown, and there are no new holes. Can he shoot through an opening that small, she wonders. She doesn't think she could. Not with any degree of accuracy. But what if he can?

Then they will die, a voice inside her says. All three of them. And you will fail.

For the first time since she picked up a gun so she could kill, Arrow feels panic. She's stuck. There's nothing she can do. There's no small moment to retreat into, no chain of events that will dictate an outcome. It's all loose and floating, and she can do only one thing. She can fire blind. But she's unwilling to do that. Or she thinks she is. It doesn't seem as though she's making a choice. She's just not doing it. If she made the decision to shoot she's not sure she would carry it out.

On the street, the girls are moving. They step out of the line of fire and lay a small bouquet of wildflowers in front of the cellist. She thinks she sees dandelions. Then they turn and walk west, toward her, and they continue down the street until they have passed her and are no longer in danger.

There's movement in the window. A change, a slight shifting in the light. A shadow behind the plastic where before there was no shadow. Her finger covers the trigger. All she needs is for him to show himself for an instant. To make a move that will tell her who he is. It's a small thing. Just another one of the small things that are not small things. The sum is almost tallied. One more movement is all it will take.

The music stops. Arrow doesn't remember having heard the last few minutes, and can't say whether the cellist has finished, or if something has happened. She keeps her focus on the fourth-floor window. Her universe consists of one square meter of plastic. And nothing happens. Nothing moves, nothing changes. Ten minutes go by. When she looks down to the street the cellist is gone.

She sinks into the floor, unsure of what has taken place. She was sure he was there. Now she isn't so sure. Why didn't he fire? He had the shot. He must have had the shot. It doesn't make sense. Why hang around for another day? A trip into enemy territory is dangerous and uncomfortable, something to be kept as short as possible. If the shot is there, you take it and get out. But he didn't.

She feels as though she's failed, though she knows she hasn't. Her job is to keep the cellist alive. Nermin said so himself in those exact terms. Whether an enemy sniper is killed is not the issue. The cellist is alive. He will be there tomorrow. So she hasn't failed.

Arrow wonders about the two girls who laid flowers in front of the cellist. Do they hate the men on the hills as much as she does? Do they hate them for being murderous bastards, killers without remorse? She hopes not. That's too easy. If they hate the men on the hills, then they are forced to hate her too. She kills just the same as they do. On days like today when she doesn't kill, she feels a loss that reveals a hostility within her that goes deeper than a lack of remorse. It's almost a lust.

She hopes that the girls, and the rest of the city, hate the men on the hills for the same reason she does. Because they made her hate. They started a war, saying that the people of Sarajevo hated each other, and the people fought back, saying they didn't, that they were a city without hatred. But then the men on the hills started to kill and mutilate and destroy. And little by little they got what they wanted, a victory as clear as it would be if they could drive their tanks through the town. They made her, and people like her, hate them.

Hours later, when it's almost dark and Arrow considers it safe to leave the apartment, she walks past the bouquet the two girls left, and sees that it's part of a larger offering of flowers that have been placed at the feet of the cellist, in the place where the shell fell. Some are wilting. She now understands what the girls were doing. What she does not understand is how it's possible that she hasn't noticed the pyre of dry flowers until now. Arrow turns away and walks toward her apartment, knowing she'll be back tomorrow.

kenan

the cellist
arrow
dragan

It is all Kenan can do to look up at what remains of the
National Library. Though the stone and brick structure still
stands, its insides are completely consumed. The fire has left
sooty licks above each window, and the domed glass ceiling
that stood proud atop the building for a century has shattered
to the floor. The tram once turned a semicircle here, offering
a comprehensive view of the iconic building. It was one of his
favorite places in the city, though he wasn't a great reader. It
was the most visible manifestation of a society he was proud
of. Now the tram tracks serve no purpose and show only what's
been lost.

The men on the hills made the library one of their first
targets, and they took to their task with great efficiency. Kenan
didn't know if it was shells that started the fire, or if someone
smuggled in a bomb as they did in the post office, but he knew
that as it burned they fired incendiary shells at it. He went
there when he heard it was burning, without knowing why. He
watched, helpless and useless, as this symbol of what the city

was and what many still wanted it to be, gave in to the desires of the men on the hills.

Fire trucks arrived, and they became targets, shot at by unseen snipers. Shells were launched at them by an army that had once sworn to protect the city. The firefighters battled the flames for as long as they could, until they were ordered back by some commander who saw the futility of the situation. Kenan saw one fireman, probably in his late twenties, stand by himself and watch the inferno rage. He didn't move at all until, exhausted, he caved in on himself, fell to his knees. His fellow firemen rushed to him, thinking a sniper had hit him. As they helped him to his feet and led him away, Kenan saw that his cheeks were streaked with sweat or tears, and his lips were moving, silent, in a way that made Kenan think he was praying. For days afterward, the ash of a million books floated down onto the city like snow.

At the time, Kenan believed the fireman was overcome by the loss of the library, but he now thinks what brought him to his knees was his inability to do anything to save it, or even slow its loss. When Kenan's children ask why this war is happening, why people are being starved and shot at, and he can't answer them, when he sees them suffering and there is nothing he can do about it, he sees the fireman in himself and he wishes someone would pick him up and carry him away. He cannot collapse, though, because his children look to him to reassure them that everything will be fine, that the war will end, that they will all survive. There are times when he doesn't know how he manages not to evaporate, how his clothes don't fall to the floor, emptied of what little substance he was filling them with.

He rounds the corner, and the Šeher Ćehaja Bridge lies ahead. He stops and adjusts his water bottles before taking shelter behind one of the library's great supporting arches. He scans the hills, not quite sure what he's looking for, but wanting some sort of reassurance that there's no one with a gun trained on the bridge. After a few minutes, a man and a woman come around the corner. They look at him, suspicious, but don't stop. They head toward the bridge, and Kenan considers calling out to them, but there's nothing he can say that will be of use. Telling them there might be a sniper watching the bridge is a little like saying the sun has come up this morning. So he lets them go. They can be his guinea pigs.

They are almost casual in their approach. They don't look up at the southern hills, they don't stop. When they reach the bridge they pick up their pace a bit, more than a fast walk but not quite a jog. The woman moves a little faster than the man, and he speeds up to stay beside her. As they near the middle of the bridge Kenan feels an overwhelming sense of doom, is sure that shots are about to come, they're both going to be killed. But the shots never come, and the couple make it to the other side. They slow down a little, perhaps feeling they're out of danger, though Kenan knows they can still be hit. They're not safe until they're behind the cover of the buildings, but the couple either don't know this or don't care.

A woman comes up behind him. She's in her early fifties, he thinks, her hair mostly gray, though that's not a good way to tell anymore. He never knew how many women put color in their hair until the war came and hair dye became another commodity for black marketeers. Kenan looks at the woman again, thinks maybe she's younger than he first thought. She might even be his age. There is no way to tell what the war has done to age her.

She has a four-liter water jug in each hand. She acknowledges Kenan, looks at the bridge. "Is it safe?"

Kenan shrugs. "A couple just went over and no one was shot. But who knows."

The woman sees his water canisters. "Are you going to the brewery?"

"Yes." For an instant Kenan wonders if she's going to ask him to get water for her, but knows even before he's done thinking it that he's being irrational. "You?"

"If I can. The hill is steep, so I stop and rest a lot. But I'll make it. It's the bridge I don't like." She looks again at the bridge, then the hills.

"I think it's safe." He considers asking her what she looks for in the hills. Maybe she knows something specific that he doesn't.

The woman doesn't respond, and Kenan gets the feeling

that he is intruding on her privacy, even though he was here first and they are in no way in a private place. He wants to be away from here, though, so he picks up his jugs and takes one last look at the bridge.

"Are you going now?" she asks, standing up straighter.

"Yes." He hesitates, unsure of what she wants from him, or if she wants anything. "Do you want to go together? You know, safety in numbers?"

She appears to be considering his proposal. He wonders which one of them is a more appealing target, then stops himself. This is no way to think.

"No," she says. "I think I'll rest here for a while."

He nods to her and steps out onto the street. He is glad to be moving along. He isn't sure what just happened, but there was something about the nature of this interaction that unnerved him. He moves as quickly as he can, a slow jog at first and then faster. His feet hit the bridge, and he knows he's now exposed. He zigzags a little, right then left then right, then runs in a straight line, attempting to create no pattern in his movements. The trick is to keep your movements random but not frenetic. He once saw a man move too quickly to the side in an attempt to be evasive, and his foot slipped out from under him and his ankle snapped. He lay in the street for several minutes until someone came and helped him to safety. Although no shot ever came it just as easily could have, and the man would have done most of the sniper's work for him.

Kenan's water bottles thump against each other, and though it's not a loud noise it sounds to him like the beating of drums, and this frightens him, makes him think someone is hunting him. He runs faster, much faster than he thinks is safe, but terror has wrapped its arms around him and he can't help himself. The end of the bridge is just ahead, and his foot catches on a cleft in the pavement. It seems like he's going to fall, but he doesn't, somehow, and he recovers himself enough to stumble across the rest of the bridge to the protection of a small building to his left.

He sits there, wheezing, his lungs hot and dry, until his breathing slows, and he pulls himself to his feet. He glances back at the library and sees the woman looking at him. It's too far for him to be sure, but he imagines she's laughing at him. She is, he realizes, using him as her guinea pig, just as he did the couple before. Did he reassure her, he wonders, or make her more reluctant to cross? She doesn't move from shelter, so he assumes he didn't instill any confidence in her.

In front of him is a café he used to go to, the Spite House. The story is that it used to be on the other side of the river, on the right bank. When the Austro-Hungarians regulated the flow of the Miljacka it was in the way, but the owner refused to allow it to be demolished. He agreed to give up his piece of land only on condition that his house be moved, brick by brick, across the river to the left bank. In addition, he demanded a bag of ducats, out of spite. Kenan's never been sure whether the story's true or not, but he doesn't think it matters. What he wants now is for the men on the hills to come down and put every building back the way it was, brick by brick. If they can cough up some money too, who is he to say what is spite and what is reparation? He looks at the now closed restaurant and laughs a little at the thought. The men on the hills will come down into the city for only one reason, and it won't be to make things the way they used to be.

He picks up his bottles, puts the rope over his shoulder, then stoops to pick up Mrs. Ristovski's bottles as well. He can't understand why she insists on these particular containers, why she can't switch to ones with handles. He knows she's old and set in her ways, but it's not as though she's been using these containers to carry water all her life. She's been dealing with the water shortage for exactly the same amount of time that he has, but without having to make the trek down a hill, through town, across a bridge, up another hill and home again. If anyone should be set in his ways it's him.

He remembers meeting her, almost seventeen years ago. He and Amila were in their early twenties, just married, their first daughter only months old. They moved into their apartment on a dreary spring morning, and in the afternoon they heard an insistent knock at the door they would come to know well.

Kenan opened up and found Mrs. Ristovski standing there,

looking much the same as she did today. She thrust a potted fern into his hands, stepped forward, removed her shoes, and looked at him.

"I am your neighbor, Mrs. Ristovski," she said. "Do you have any slippers?"

Kenan introduced himself, handed the plant to his bemused wife, and rooted through several boxes until he found a pair of slippers.

"They're a little small," she said as she jammed her feet into them, "but they'll do for now. Next time I'll bring my own."

They sat on the sofa Kenan's parents had given them as a wedding present while his wife made them coffee. Mrs. Ristovski gave him a long list of do's and don'ts regarding the fern, which he listened to as attentively as he could. The baby was sleeping in the next room. He mentioned her presence several times and spoke in a soft voice, hoping Mrs. Ristovski would follow suit. But she grew louder every time she spoke, until it seemed to Kenan that she was shouting.

His wife returned with the coffee just as the baby woke, screaming. She scowled at him, as though it was his fault Mrs. Ristovski couldn't keep her voice down. When Amila was gone, Mrs. Ristovski took a small sip of her coffee and wrinkled up her face. "That's quite a holler your baby has. I hope you and your wife aren't as loud."

Kenan assured her they were not, and the rest of the visit passed more or less without incident. She returned once or twice a week from then on, usually in the evenings when Kenan was home. He followed her instructions about the fern as well as he could, but it deteriorated rapidly in his care. This did not escape Mrs. Ristovski's notice. On a subsequent visit, she looked at the dead fern, shook her head, and said, "I hope you're better with children than you are with plants. They are considerably more difficult."

Kenan later learned that every time someone moved into the building, Mrs. Ristovski brought them a fern that without exception died a few weeks later. The common opinion was that it had somehow been poisoned, doomed from the beginning, but Kenan never really believed it. He had, however, noticed that her apartment itself had no plants of any kind.

He often found himself defending her to others, halfheartedly, reminding them that her husband had died fifty years ago and she'd been alone ever since. But the more he thought about it, the less that seemed a good reason for her bitterness. She couldn't have been more than twenty-five when she was widowed, which was certainly young enough to begin a life again. He didn't have a clue what had made her the way she was, if it was losing her husband in the war, the war itself, or something that happened after. Maybe she was always like this.

None of this explains why he is here with her impossible bottles today, he knows. He made her a promise, but he has broken promises to others and suspects he will again. He can't even pretend to like her, and while he is a little afraid of her, he isn't so intimidated that he needs to bow to her every wish. If he is honest with himself, he has no idea why he keeps bringing Mrs. Ristovski water.

It's time to get moving. The brewery isn't much farther, just a bit west and then south up the hill. He crosses the street and cuts through an empty lot, taking cover where he can find it. As he climbs the hill, water runs down the street from the taps at the brewery. The trail of those who have come before him reminds Kenan of the traces slugs leave in a garden. A truck with an enormous plastic tank in the back passes him, honks its horn, forcing him to the side of the road. There are a lot more people in the street now, most laden with the paraphernalia of water collection, and they too are forced to the side of the road for this truck and several others that follow soon after. It is a pilgrimage, a parade, all of them rats of Hamelin. When the bright-red hulk of the brewery comes into view, he feels both happy and apprehensive, because although he has at last arrived at his destination, he knows he has a long way to go before he is home again.

the cellist
arrow
kenan

dragan

"*Do you think,*" Dragan asks, "it's worse to be wounded or killed?"

He's not sure why he asked Emina this question. It seems almost frivolous, like asking if it's better to be boiled alive using water or cooking oil.

He leans against the boxcar, and she faces him, her back to the street. Every so often she shifts her weight from one foot to the other, as though she can't find a comfortable way to stand.

"I think," she says, her eyes moving toward the intersection, "it's better to be wounded. At least that way you have a chance to live."

"It's not much of a chance," he says, wondering why. What possible point could there be to this conversation? But the words keep on coming out of him, and he can't seem to stop. It's like picking at a scab.

"What do you mean? A chance is a chance."

"There's not a whole lot the hospitals can do for you.

They're low on supplies, low on people." He doesn't know for sure that either of these things is true, but it seems likely.

"I think they're fairly well equipped. It seems a lot of people are wounded and don't die." He can see that his criticism bothers her, that she doesn't want him to be right. Her neck has got red, and she's moved away from him, ever so slightly.

"If they're so well equipped, then why are you risking your life to deliver medicine that's almost a decade old?"

He's scored a direct hit. She steps back, takes her hands out of her pockets and raises them to her chest. For an instant Dragan wonders if she's about to strike him. He wouldn't mind if she did. He knows he deserves it.

"I'm sorry," he says. "I don't know why I said that."

She doesn't move. She stares hard at him without blinking. He doesn't know what she's looking for. He tries to appear contrite, tells himself not to say anything, to be quiet. Nothing he can say is going to fix this.

Yet he feels his mouth moving, and words are coming out of him. "I don't understand how you're not scared. I don't understand how the idea of being shot or blown apart doesn't scare you."

She breathes out, lets her hands drop to her side. "There is a man playing the cello in the street," she says. "Near the market. Where the people were killed lining up for bread."

Dragan heard about the massacre when it happened. It wasn't far from his sister's house. If he didn't bring bread home each day he worked, it is possible she would have been in that line. But he hadn't thought about it since. While it was one of the worst individual incidents, it wasn't much more than the overall death toll each day.

"Every day, at four o'clock." She turns toward him as she says this, as if there's something he doesn't understand. "Every day he sits there and plays. People go and listen. Some leave flowers. I've been several times. Sometimes I listen all the way through, and sometimes I leave after only a few minutes."

Dragan nods. He has heard of the cellist, in passing, but has never given him much thought, and has never been to see him. He's unsure why Emina is telling him all this, but he won't interrupt her. He will let her speak until she's finished.

"I don't know the piece he plays, what its name is. It's a sad tune. But it doesn't make me sad." She's looking right at him, not looking away, and he's a little uncomfortable. "Why do you suppose he's there? Is he playing for the people who died? Or is he playing for the people who haven't? What does he hope to accomplish?"

Dragan realizes this isn't a rhetorical question. She expects an answer. He doesn't have one. He has no idea what would possess a person to do such a thing.

"Who is he playing for?" she asks again, and suddenly Dragan thinks he knows.

"Maybe he's playing for himself," he says. "Maybe it's all he knows how to do, and he's not doing it to make something happen." And he thinks this is true. What the cellist wants isn't a change, or to set things right again, but to stop things from getting worse. Because, as the optimist in Emina's mother's joke said, it can always get worse. But perhaps the only thing that will stop it from getting worse is people doing the things they know how to do.

His answer appears to have satisfied Emina, or at least intrigued her. She leans back against the boxcar. After a while, she says, "Jovan says he's crazy. He says it's an act of futility, that he's going to get himself killed."

Dragan considers this. "Jovan's a fool," he says. He doesn't look at Emina, stares straight ahead.

"I know," she says. "I used to sort of like that about him."

He risks a glance at her and sees she isn't smiling. "I'm afraid, Dragan. I'm afraid of everything, of dying, of not dying. I'm afraid that it will stay like this forever, that this war isn't a war, but just how life will be."

Dragan nods. The fight has gone out of him. "Me too," he says. "Everything."

She takes a step forward, turns and stands beside him. So far no one has been brave enough to try crossing again, but it looks as if someone will soon make a move, and everyone seems to be waiting to see what will happen. Dragan looks up at the sky and watches a large gray cloud. It appears to him that the cloud is moving slowly. He wonders if this is the case or if it's a matter of perspective, if the cloud is in fact moving as fast as a bird can fly or a car can drive. He doesn't think so, but there's no way to tell, and the fact that there's no way to tell comforts him. He looks back to the street, making a point not to look skyward again until he's sure the cloud is gone.

A man wearing a yellow jacket decides it's safe enough to cross. He darts forward, keeping his head low, and zigzags his way safely to the other side. This seems to bring a measure of relief to the people waiting, and a few more work up the nerve to move. They make it to the other side without anything happening. Gradually the backlog of people who have been lingering disappears, until there's no one left in the shelter of the boxcar who was there the last time the sniper fired, except for Dragan and Emina.

"A woman has a friend come to visit," Emina says, her voice quick and light. "The friend comes in, and the woman asks if she would like a coffee. 'No,' the friend says, 'thanks, I'm fine.' The woman says, 'Great, now I can take a shower.'"

Dragan laughs, even though he's heard the joke before. There are a half-dozen variations on it, but in each one the woman manages to do something large with an absurdly small amount of water. It's not far from the truth. Dragan is now able to wash his whole body with half a liter of water. A quarter to wash, a quarter to rinse. It's not the same, but it works. It's a treat if the water is warm.

In a few weeks, his son Davor will turn nineteen. If he were still here he would almost certainly have become involved in the fighting, either voluntarily or as a conscript. Dragan can remember the day his son was born, in the early hours of the morning, the sun not yet up. They had been at the hospital for a day and a half. His wife was in labor for nearly thirty-six hours, and the worried faces of the doctors and nurses had him terrified, but then his son was pulled free of his wife's body and declared healthy. His small cry emerging from a bundle of blankets sounded to Dragan like music. Afterward he had an overwhelming feeling of benevolence, not just for his son, but for the world around him, wishing it were everything it wasn't, wondering what he could do to make things better. But the feeling faded, and then it was gone entirely, like it had never happened.

Dragan still wanted the best for his son, and he still wanted the world to be different, but he never really thought about how he could accomplish this, what possible effect his actions could have. Now he often wonders whether there was anything he did or didn't do that played some small part in his city's disintegration. He wonders what would have happened if the men on the hills and the men in the city had in their hearts a tiny fraction of the benevolence felt for and known by a small child.

Approaching from the east, about twenty meters away, is a small black dog. It has its nose to the ground, its tail low, and it moves with a determined gait. The dog doesn't stop to smell any particular spot or greet any people as they pass. Dragan finds himself watching it getting closer and closer, and when he looks at Emina he sees she's doing the same. The dog passes by them, close enough to touch, but doesn't acknowledge their existence. No one else on the street seems to have noticed it, but why should they? The city is full of stray dogs. There's nothing special about this one. If that is so, he thinks, then why are Emina and I both watching? It's because of the singularity of the dog's intent. This dog has somewhere to go.

The dog reaches the intersection and enters it without hesitation. He wonders if it knows that there's a man with a gun on the hills. As if to answer his question, the dog lifts its nose from the ground, turns its head to the left, and glances up into the hills. This makes Dragan believe the dog knows what's going on. It may even know where the sniper is. Perhaps a dog can smell a bullet's path, trace its trajectory back to the source. The dog could very well know which window or rooftop the sniper shoots from. Has anyone ever tested this? Do we know for sure what a dog can and can't smell?

Dragan wonders if a sniper would shoot a dog. Would he waste a bullet, and risk revealing his position to a counter-sniper? If the men on the hills will not shoot at a dog, but they will shoot at us, this must mean they consider us different. But the question is whether we are better or worse. Do they recognize more of themselves in a dog or in a human?

The dog is nearly across the intersection now, its nose to the ground. It reaches the other side and then, unexpectedly, it stops, turns around, and looks back. It stares at the street for a few seconds, at what Dragan can't tell, and then continues on, until it's out of sight.

"Where do you suppose that dog was off to?" Emina asks him.

He turns to her, sees she's smiling. "I have no idea."

"I wonder what urgent task a dog would have to make it move so deliberately?"

Dragan is about to answer when he realizes that wherever it is going, whatever task it's engaged with, there's little difference between him and the dog. They are both only trying to survive. Unlike the men on the hills, who still make a distinction between humans and dogs, Dragan now sees little difference. He felt the same amount of concern for the dog when it was in the sniper's line of fire as he did for the forty or fifty people who have crossed this intersection since he's been here.

Emina is looking at him, waiting for an answer to her question.

"Where do any of us have to go that's so urgent?" he says, hoping this will end the discussion. He doesn't want to think about the dog anymore.

He wonders how long he's been here, waiting to cross. Perhaps three quarters of an hour. Has this time waiting increased or decreased his chances of making it?

"Why did the Sarajevan cross the road?" he asks Emina.

She shakes her head, takes her hands out of her pockets, and brushes her hair out of her face. "That's a good question."

"To get to the other side," he answers. Emina groans, because it really is a bad joke. Dragan doesn't care. He hasn't told a joke in months. It feels good, even if the joke is awful.

"I think," she says, still half laughing, "it's time for this Sarajevan to act like a chicken. If I go now, I might make it back in time to hear the cellist."

Dragan stops laughing. She's right. They've been here long enough. "I'll go with you," he says.

Emina nods, and they move toward the street, with her in front, Dragan following. When they're almost at the end of the boxcar, at the spot where they will have to run, Dragan begins to lose his nerve. His hands sweat, and then his back and feet. He feels short of breath. He reaches out and places his hand on Emina's shoulder, stopping her.

"I can't yet," he says. "I'm not ready."

Emina nods. "Do you want me to wait with you?"

He does, but he doesn't want to tell her this. "I'm okay," he says. "I'm not in any special hurry."

She looks at him, her face tense, and he wonders if she's going to decide to stay with him despite his reassurances.

"Give Raza my love," she says, leaning in and hugging him. She feels warm and substantial, much larger than when he hugged her only a short time ago. She has become real to him again. She is the person he once knew. Affected by the war, changed, but the woman he knew is still in there. She hasn't been covered in the gray that colors the streets. He wonders why he hasn't seen this before, wonders how much else he hasn't seen.

Two people are crossing from the other side, a man and a woman. The man is about halfway through the intersection, the woman just beginning. The woman's hair is tied back with a black scarf, and the man wears a brown hat with a peak, a type of hat Dragan has never owned but has always thought looked good. It's the sort of hat a detective might wear, he thinks.

Emina steps into the street. She begins to accelerate into a run, but it seems to Dragan that she slows down. The whole world has become muddled, sticky, like it's underwater. The blue wool of Emina's coat is a blur, and Dragan feels tired. He could sleep for days.

A young man comes up beside Dragan, gets ready to cross. He hesitates for only an instant, taking one deep breath and moving forward. As he steps into the street Emina is thrown to the side with a violent surge, and the sound of gunfire punches through silence. The man in the hat stops for an instant and then runs toward Dragan. The woman turns back, hoping to retreat the way she came. Emina lies still, not moving. Dragan can't see where she's been hit, if she's alive or not.

Beside him the half-dozen or so people who are in the vicinity rush ahead, toward the edge of the boxcar, their eyes on the street. A few shout to those in the sniper's line of fire, yelling for them to run and other obvious ideas.

The young man moves forward toward Emina. He should be turning back, Dragan thinks. He's going the wrong way. Then Dragan understands what he's doing, and he wants to go with the man, to help him and see if Emina can be saved. But his feet don't move. Around him everyone is alive with a frenzied energy, but he hasn't stirred an inch.

The young man and the man in the hat reach Emina at the same time, just as the woman makes it to safety. Dragan sees people on the opposite side of the street rush to her, to see if she's all right, though it's clear she is. The young man bends down, puts his arms around Emina. The man in the hat keeps running, doesn't stop. The young man looks up in disbelief as he goes by, shouts out to him for help. If he hears, the man in the hat gives no indication. Just as he's about to reach the safety of the boxcar there's another shot. The man's hat flies off his head and lands at Dragan's feet. Dragan stares down at the hat, which has landed upside down on the pavement. He can see from the label that it was made in Vienna. He looks ahead. The hat's owner is lying on his stomach.

Around him, people realize that the sniper is able to fire far closer to the edge of the boxcar than they'd thought. They duck down, all of them except Dragan, and he's reminded of the way a flock of birds can turn in unison while in flight, as though programmed. Then a hand grabs at him. He understands he's in danger, and gets down on the ground with the others. They move back, staying as low as they can, until they're away from the street, about three meters from the man who no longer has a hat.

The young man has picked Emina up, and Dragan sees she's alive. One of her arms hangs down, her sleeve soaked in blood, but her eyes are open and her good hand holds tight around the shoulder of her rescuer. A bullet strikes the pavement a few feet in front of them. The young man doesn't react, continues undaunted, slow and awkward, and Dragan doesn't think he's going to make it.

As they pass the hatless man, who Dragan assumes is dead, a hand reaches up to them, weak and imploring. The hatless man is somehow still alive, though it seems he's unable to move. The young man ignores him, keeps moving. Emina looks down at him, says nothing, and then looks away.

Dragan tries to count the seconds since the sniper last fired, tries to figure out how much time they have before the next bullet comes. He doesn't know how long it's been, however, and has no idea how long it will take for the sniper to aim and fire again.

Emina and the young man are two meters from him, and then one, and then they're there. They tumble to the ground behind him, and he hears Emina cry out. Dragan doesn't turn around. He can't look away from the street, where the hatless man is trying to crawl, a centimeter at a time, to safety. There's an expanding smear of blood surrounding him, and although Dragan knows the street around him is full of noise, he doesn't hear a sound. He counts under his breath, hears slow numbers tick in his own voice. When he gets to eight, the hatless man's head bursts, the top of his skull evaporating in a fine red drizzle punctuated by the thunderclap of a rifle echoing down the hill.

Dragan looks down and sees that the hat is in his hands. He doesn't remember picking it up, has no idea why he'd do such a thing. He looks at the hat, runs his thumb along the brim, and then he leans down and sets it on the asphalt before turning to Emina.

A night spent drifting between sleep and a replay of the day's events leaves Arrow with little rest and no further insight into what happened. None of it seems to fit into any scenario she can invent. She's absolutely certain that the sniper was there, and that he had a shot at the cellist. But otherwise nothing makes sense. This worries her. She's beginning to think perhaps she has lost her way, perhaps she isn't the weapon she was just a few days ago. She's also forced to consider the likelihood that the sniper the men on the hills have sent is much better at his job than most. And maybe he has a plan that is beyond her reach.

It's nearly nine in the morning, and again she sits in the spot where the cellist will play. But something has changed. Where yesterday she sat with her back straight and her eyes alert to the street around her, today her shoulders sag and pull her spine into a curve. She stares at the ground in front of her feet.

She thinks about the funeral she attended last month. When her neighbor Slavko was killed by a sniper on his way back from collecting water, shot clean through the neck, they took him to the Koševo Stadium, now made into a burial ground. His wife thought he'd like to be buried near to where he'd enjoyed so many football matches.

Arrow doesn't normally go to funerals. In the early days of the war she went to as many as she could, out of respect, but then she became numb to them, and the more she attended the less she felt, until the misery of death and the sorrow of those left alive made her angry. When she looked at the faces of the husbands and wives and mothers and sons left behind, she felt a rage build inside her, and she felt that rage directed especially at those at the funeral who appeared most bereaved. How could they possibly feel so much grief? How could they not have reached the point months and months ago at which a person simply can't feel any more pain? And then, just as she was sure she was about to walk up to a weeping widower and snap his neck, she would recognize what she was doing and thinking, and she would be ashamed. How had she become such a person? Then she would remember the men on the hills, and she would know that it was they who had done this. Later that day, or the next, she would kill as many of them as possible. But the process left her exhausted, and it became an expenditure of energy she could no longer afford. She didn't need to go looking for reasons to send bullets into the hills.

But she had liked Slavko. He had retired just before the war from the city's parks department, and he knew a lot about animals and birds. As they waited for the elevator, he often told her about interesting things he had seen. He was tall and thin and wore large glasses that made him look like a bug. As a young girl, Arrow had often thought of him as a giant grasshopper. Once, when she was kicking a ball in the street with some of the other children in the neighborhood, the ball got away from them and Slavko, who was walking up the street, stopped it from going down the hill. He held it against the curb, looked at the group of them, and then, with a leg that was far too long, kicked it to her. She wasn't the nearest child to him, and he certainly knew all of them. She knew that he had chosen her, and when the ball skipped past the other children in a straight line ending at her feet she felt a rush of pride. "Watch out for cars," he said to the group of them, and as he walked by her he put his hand on her shoulder. "And have fun."

So when his wife knocked on her door and asked her to come to Slavko's funeral, a request that was unheard of for a bereaved widow to make, she couldn't refuse. "He always liked talking with you," Ismira said. They never had any children themselves.

"Of course I'll come," Arrow said, and this seemed to make Ismira happy. The funeral was the next day, and as she stood in the converted football field with two dozen other people, she felt the familiar anger begin to build within her. She tried to think of something else, directing her attention away from the mourners. A row of newly dug graves led away from the hole they placed Slavko in. They gaped, empty and expectant, like the mouths of baby birds. She knew that by the end of the week they'd all be full.

A fat man stood next to her. She'd never met him, but the presence of anyone who was overweight was remarkable in it-self. Most people had lost ten or twenty kilograms since the siege began. She didn't know how a person could remain fat when there was nothing to eat. Then she remembered that for some people, those with connections and privileges, plenty of food was available. She assumed that this man must be some sort of gangster, or perhaps a corrupt government official. She wondered what a person like that was doing at Slavko's funeral. She didn't think he'd traveled in those circles.

As she turned to get a better look at the fat man she heard a familiar whistling and knew that a shell was headed for them. Others knew this as well, but there was nothing she could do for them. She saw immediately there was no cover to be had. The only real protection possible was the open graves, and al-though her mind demanded she hurl herself into one she did not comply. She threw herself to the ground, and for the first time in months smelled sweet wet grass. A shell exploded be-hind her, not far away, and she heard the fat man beside her begin to cry. His sobs were drowned out by another shell strik-ing, this one slightly farther away.

Arrow lay on her stomach until the shelling stopped. When she lifted her head everyone but herself and the fat man was gone. He was alive, shaking, and she couldn't see any sign that he was hurt. At first she thought that everyone else was dead. She thought the men on the hills had invented some new weapon that could make people disappear. No unpleasant carnage for the world to see. No evidence whatsoever. It would be as if they had never even existed. Then she saw a head emerge from one of the graves, and then another, until people began to climb out of the open graves. She watched as some men helped Ismira and another woman out of Slavko's grave.

The fat man sat up, tried to get to his feet, failed. He exhaled a long wheeze and looked at her.

"Why didn't you go into a grave?" she asked him, surprised by how harsh her voice sounded.

His face relaxed a little. "I was afraid I wouldn't be able to get out," he said. "If you think I'm big now, you should have seen me before."

Arrow stood and helped the fat man to his feet. "How did you know Slavko?"

"I didn't, really. We were waiting in line for water. He helped me when I dropped my canister." The fat man looked at his feet. "Why didn't you go in a grave?" he asked, raising his face to her.

She smiled. "I was worried you might land on top of me," she said, and the man grinned back. Later, though, she knew the real reason. She would not let the men on the hills decide when she went below the ground. If she were to go underground it would be because she decided to or because they killed her. But she wasn't going to do their work for them. She wasn't going to live in a grave.

Arrow's not sure why this memory has come to her now. She doesn't see a connection with the day's problem. She looks at the pile of decaying flowers at her feet and is reminded of the job she's here to do.

She looks up at the window where she believes the sniper hides. It's a perfect spot. Hitting the cellist from there would be no challenge at all. She looks to the west, to where her own hiding spot is, and she looks above her, where her trap is. All is as it should be. There's no problem with her plan.

She gets to her feet and is about to turn west when her legs go stiff and her fingers begin to throb. She freezes, trying to figure out what has prompted this reaction in her. She breathes in deep and then she realizes that the sniper is watching her. She doesn't know where he is, but she can feel his eyes on her. He could be in any window, or he could be one of ten people who are in view and appear to be engaged in legitimate affairs. It doesn't matter, really, because she doesn't have her rifle with her. Initially this causes her to panic, but then she thinks that not having the rifle may have saved her. To him, she's just another person sitting in the street. He may assume she's a relative of someone who died here, or another citizen come to pay her respects, or an admirer of the cellist. How would he know she's the one who has been sent to kill him?

Of course she knows that if he were watching her at just the right moment, when she looked up at his window, and then to hers, and then above her, he would know everything. But what would he do with that information? She thinks that if he knew who she was she'd be dead by now.

To be safe, she puts her hands in her pockets and heads east, away from the building she uses. She walks past his window and down the street, not looking back, not really looking anywhere. She continues east until she hits the burned-out ruins of the library. She then heads north, and backtracks toward her apartment to retrieve the rifle she will use to kill her enemy.

She has decided to give this sniper the benefit of the doubt. She will assume he's as good as, if not better than, she is. She will take all the necessary precautions to avoid detection. Though she's been in this apartment for nearly five hours, she won't enter her line of fire for a few more minutes, until just before four o'clock. She won't even give him a chance of spotting her. She's already gone to the decoy apartment and repositioned her dummy rifle and hat, so if he notices them he won't have the opportunity to see that the gun he thinks is looking for him is in the exact same position as the day before.

She didn't report in to Nermin last night. He will know that she hasn't killed the sniper, but he will also know that the cellist is still alive. At the end of today, if she lives, she'll have to see him. She isn't sure how it will go if she doesn't get the sniper or, worse, if the cellist dies. She's never failed before, and she would rather not find out how her army views such failures.

It's time. Soon the cellist will enter the street and the sniper will be forced to show himself. She moves toward the window, rests her rifle on an overturned table to help steady it, and brings her eye to the scope. She locates the fourth-floor window where he will be and looks for the hole in the plastic. It's easy to spot, having grown in size since the last time she saw it up close. It's now more than large enough to aim and fire through, and Arrow is confident that when the sniper attempts to do so, she'll have a clear and straightforward shot at him. It will be nothing to send him a bullet. She smiles.

The cellist steps out of the doorway and walks to his spot in the middle of the street. Nothing happens in the fourth-floor window. He unfolds his stool and sits, motionless and silent. He lifts his arms and begins to play. Still nothing happens in the fourth-floor window. Arrow realizes that she's beginning to know the notes he plays. She's able to hear them in her mind before she hears them with her ears, to fill in those that are drowned out by the street and the shells and her own concentration.

After five minutes she knows something is wrong. The cellist plays for only ten or fifteen minutes at the most, and the sniper hasn't shown yet. There's no reason she can think of for him to delay, at least none that doesn't result in the disintegration of her plans. But she has no choice other than to keep the fourth-floor window in her scope, to wait for him to move. She has, somehow, through her series of decisions, put herself into a position where there's no alternative to the path she's chosen. The choices she's made have left her without choice.

There's movement in the decoy apartment. She senses it before she sees it, long before she repositions her rifle barrel forty degrees to the north. When she looks through the scope she doesn't see anything out of the ordinary. Everything appears unchanged. She suspects her mind of playing tricks on her and turns her attention back to the fourth-floor window.

Her eye is just adjusting to the change in her scope's position when she grasps what has changed in the decoy apartment. The rifle she saw isn't the one she put there. She has fallen into her own trap. And, though she doesn't see it, she knows that the rifle in the window has now found her, and a bullet is on its way. She hits the ground as it rips the plastic and punches through the wall at the back of the room. She clutches her knees to her chest and waits for a second shot, the one that will kill the cellist.

The music continues. The echo of the shot sent for her bounces through the buildings on either side of the street and drowns the cellist out, but once it dissipates, his cello emerges again, and there is no second shot. He plays on to the end, either oblivious to or unconcerned about the gunshot that came from less than a dozen meters above him. Of course he would have no way of knowing which side fired the shot, Arrow knows. She wonders whether he cares who fires what bullets. She wonders how much it matters to anyone.

She resists the urge to pick up her gun and attempt to fire back. For some reason the sniper hasn't killed the cellist. She suspects he isn't convinced she's dead, and is unwilling to move his sights from her window. Arrow stays still. She wants him to believe she's dead.

"I think either he evacuated after the first shot, or else he was waiting to see if he'd hit you," Nermin says. "Or maybe he didn't have a clear shot at the cellist." He leans back in his chair as he says this, as though the act of relaxing indicates a conclusion reached.

Arrow knows he had a clear shot, and she doesn't think he fled or was waiting to confirm her death. This feeling has been growing in her ever since she left the apartment. She has no idea why he didn't kill the cellist, however, and isn't eager to tell Nermin anything about what she does or does not think.

"I'll put a man in that apartment overnight, in case he comes looking for a body."

"Make sure he stays away from the window, and that he's gone by morning," she says. "He'll be watching, and he knows what I look like."

"Of course," Nermin says. He stares at her like he's considering something, and then, appearing to have reached a decision, he leans forward. Arrow thinks he looks tired. There are deep creases around his eyes she can't remember seeing before, and his fatigues, usually crisp and clean, are wrinkled and stained.

"The situation here is uncertain," he says. "I know I have made promises to you, and I will attempt to keep them, but there are things going on internally that may make it difficult for both of us in the days to come."

She nods. It's no secret that there's a struggle between those who would defend the city at all costs and those who feel that the principles of the city, the ideas that made Sarajevo worth fighting for, cannot and should not be abandoned in the fight to save it. In the middle are the criminals. When the war first started they were the only ones who knew how to fight, really fight, and they leapt to defend the city. Now they are uncontrollable, and it has become harder and harder for those who aren't criminals to overlook the profiteering and lawlessness and other abuses. But power is rarely given up voluntarily. It's a question of who will prevail. She knows the survival of the city depends as much on the attitude of the defenders as it does on repelling the attackers. A city of zealots and criminals isn't worth saving.

She sees, for the first time, that Nermin is in a difficult position. The autonomy he has granted her does not fit in with the plans of those who are angling for power. An entity like her, a killer you can't control, is a dangerous thing. It would be different if she were simply good at her job. In that case few would even notice her existence. Perhaps this is what Nermin thought would happen when he sought her out. But her abilities are a known quantity, difficult to disguise. If Nermin is involved in a power struggle, she's a liability to him.

"Am I in danger?" she asks, knowing she probably is.

Nermin smiles. "Of course you are," he says. "There are men on the hills with guns. Only hours ago one of them tried to kill you."

His joke bothers her, and she tells him so. He folds his hands on his desk. She notices his fingernails need cutting.

"There is a lot less tolerance for tolerance right now. I hope this will change. If it doesn't, we will both be in a dangerous situation. We need to resolve this cellist business. What happens after that is beyond our control."

He stands, and Arrow understands she's dismissed. As she leaves the office she's struck by the distinct feeling that the next time she sees Nermin Filipović the world as they each know it will be entirely different.

When morning comes Arrow doesn't go to the street. Now that her adversary is aware of her, now that he knows who she is, she can't risk being spotted. Besides, there's nothing in the street she hasn't already seen. The only thing she's curious about is whether the pile of flowers has grown.

She's becoming frustrated with how much she doesn't know. Until recently she didn't have this problem. She thinks maybe it all started with the cellist, but can't remember exactly. So she can't even answer the question of when her questions ceased having answers. She shakes her head at this, stifles a frustrated smirk. She won't succumb to the lure of black humor. She's spent too much time with Nermin and doesn't like it.

Her plan for the day is simple. She's reasonably confident that the sniper will think she's dead. She knows she probably should be. So he will be unlikely to spend too much time worrying about the apartment where she was hiding. No sniper ever returns to the same place twice, particularly a place where someone else was killed. If he thinks she's alive he'll assume she'd find another spot, and if he assumes she's dead he'll know that the next person they send will avoid the scene of his predecessor's failure.

She has, in a small concession to how risky her strategy is, switched windows and set up one room to the east, in what used to be the master bedroom. Part of the windowsill is missing, likely caused by the shell that has obliterated the contents of the room. There's a hole about sixty centimeters wide extending from the sill into the floor, and the plastic covering the window stretches over it but isn't fastened securely. It's a simple matter to slip the barrel of her rifle into the hole, pushing aside the plastic enough to have a clear shot at most of the street to the east. She's invisible here, and as she waits for the day to pass it occurs to her that this is the place she should have chosen to begin with, and that bothers her. She hasn't done what a weapon would have.

The day goes slowly. She hears heavy shelling to the west, in the direction of Dobrinja and Mojmilo. A part of her wishes she could be there. She thinks of the people who, because she has been here for the past three days, she has not shot. Men who hate her, men who would kill her, men who have killed people like her in the last three days because she did not kill them first.

But then she begins to wonder even about this. Do the men on the hills hate her? Or do they hate the idea of her, because she's different from them, and that in this difference there might be some sort of inferiority or superiority that is hers or theirs, that in the end threatens the potential happiness of everyone? She begins to wonder whether they fight against an idea, and that fight manifests itself as hatred. If so, they are no different from her. Except for one key detail that simply can't be ignored or pushed aside. The idea she felt prepared to give her life for was not one that could include the hatred she feels for the men on the hills. The Sarajevo she fought for was one where you didn't have to hate a person because of what they were. It didn't matter what you were, what your ancestors had been, or what your children would be. You could hate a person for what they did. You could hate a murderer, you could hate a rapist, and you could hate a thief. This is what first drove her to kill the men on the hills, because they were all these things. But now, she knows, she's driven mainly by a hatred of them, the idea of them as a group, and not by their actions.

This realization stuns her, and she feels an impulse to leave her rifle where it lies and return to her apartment. But she doesn't. She stays where she is. At four o'clock the cellist comes out and her finger tightens around the trigger.

The sniper shows himself almost immediately. He's in a second-storey window, one of the three she first suspected. As the cellist begins to play, the sniper appears through a hole in the plastic, one that wasn't there before and isn't very well hidden. Arrow is surprised by how easy it is to spot him.

The sniper puts the cellist in his sights. Arrow is about to send a bullet into him, but stops. His finger isn't on the trigger. This isn't a detail she would usually notice, or care about, but she can see it in her scope, and it makes her pause. His hand isn't even in the vicinity of the trigger. His right hand holds the uppermost point of the stock, and his shot is clear, but his left hand isn't on his rifle. It hangs down to his side, out of her view.

She wonders whether he can hear the music. He's not much farther from the cellist than she is, so he must. Does it sound the same to him? What does he hear? What does he think about this man who sits in the street and plays?

For several minutes, Arrow does nothing. She watches the sniper through the scope of her rifle and listens to the music lift off the street. It makes her sad. A heavy, slow kind of sad, the sort that does not bring you to tears but makes you feel like crying. It is, she thinks, the worst feeling there could be.

Her finger is still on the trigger. If he moves, she will fire. But he does not move. The music is nearly finished, and he hasn't shifted a millimeter. She begins to doubt herself, wonders if he's real, if it's possible he's a decoy. But then he moves, and she knows what she sees is a person.

His head leans back slightly, and she sees that his eyes are closed, that he's no longer looking through his scope. She knows what he's doing. It's very clear to her, unmistakable. He's listening to the music. And then Arrow knows why he didn't fire yesterday.

She wants him to move his hand, to make a move that will decide for her what she will do. Because she is, at once, sure of two things. The first is that she does not want to kill this man, and the second is that she must.

Time is running out. There's no reason not to kill him. A sniper of his ability has without doubt killed dozens, if not hundreds. Not just soldiers. Women crossing streets. Children in playgrounds. Old men in water lines. She knows this to a certainty. Yet she doesn't want to pull her trigger. All because she can see that he doesn't want to pull his.

He hasn't moved. He still sits with his eyes closed, one hand on the stock of his rifle, the other at his side. The final notes of the cellist's melody reach him, and he smiles. His eyes open, and a small hole erupts between them. The back of his head disintegrates and the gray viscus of his brain slaps onto the wall behind him. He falls from sight and his rifle falls on top of him.

Arrow lowers her rifle and looks down at the street. The cellist has finished. He picks up his stool and cello and heads for his door. He pauses just before he enters, and she wonders if he will look in her direction. Even though he can't possibly see her, she wants him to turn toward her, to acknowledge her in some way. The cellist adjusts his grip on his instrument and disappears into the building.

kenan

The brewery has been badly damaged and parts of it are no longer safe, but its springs are deep beneath the surface, and the basement of the building is impenetrable even to the men on the hills, though that hasn't stopped them from trying to level the bright-red building. The brewery is situated in a vulnerable position, only a short distance from the occupied hills. There have been several mortar attacks here already. So far none of them has happened on days when Kenan was present.

Outside, there are about a hundred people in line for water. Kenan has been here when the line had as many as three hundred people, and he's happy that he won't have to wait for hours today. Water hoses coming out to the street from the brewery feed large pipes set up off the ground on supports, which in turn have smaller hoses branching off from them. Kenan estimates about twenty people at a time can get water, and most have roughly as many canisters as he does, so it shouldn't be too long before it's his turn. People move forward at a steady pace, though it seems that just as one person leaves with their water another enters the line.

There's a man at the front of the line who has a dog with him. It's a medium-sized dog, some sort of terrier with curly brownish fur. There's a thermos tied to its collar, and before the man fills up his bottles he takes the lid off the thermos and fills it. He places it on the ground, and as he fills his four large canisters the dog laps up the water in the thermos lid as though it was a race, which, Kenan supposes, it is. When the man is finished filling his canisters he fills the terrier's thermos and puts on the lid. Not a drop is left in it. He ties the thermos to the dog's collar and begins to load his canisters into the make-shift dolly he's using to transport them.

Kenan has considered using a dolly, but decided that there was too much debris on the street that might clog its wheels and make it difficult to maneuver, slowing him down. Now, though, seeing how much water the man is able to transport, he wonders whether he might try one on his next trip. If he could fill his two backup containers, and maybe find a couple more somewhere, he wouldn't have to make the trip as often.

At the taps, people try to move as quickly as they can. No one wants to linger, but it's a rare opportunity to be out and among others, so some of them can't help themselves from taking perhaps a bit longer than they need. He hears the sound of water and people and the engines of large trucks that haul water to who knows where, maybe the troops on the front. If he forgets why he's there, he can almost imagine everything is normal, that this is an everyday street scene. He tries to let his eyes go a little out of focus, tries to believe he's at an outdoor market. People are talking about a concert or a football match. It's a good feeling, but it lasts for only an instant, because a woman is shouting at him to take his place at a vacated tap.

After a muttered apology he steps forward. The water pours from the pipes, slapping onto the pavement at his feet. Kenan has never understood why they don't have a valve on each outlet to shut off the water between users. It seems to him an awful waste of such a precious resource. He has risked his life to get this water, water he can't get anywhere else, and here it is running into the ground as though it doesn't matter. Perhaps they can't get the necessary plumbing, or perhaps it has something to do with the pumps, or perhaps the supply of water underneath the brewery is so vast that it's more trouble than it's worth. He hopes someone has done their homework, that they're absolutely certain the water will keep running.

He leans down until his containers are on the ground, steps out of the rope that runs over each shoulder and across the back of his neck. He kneels, places Mrs. Ristovski's containers in front of him and unties his own. With a sharp twist he removes the caps and places them in a neat pile. His bottles are lined up at his left, two rows of four. He flexes his hands, takes a deep breath, moves his shoulders in a circle three times until he feels his muscles loosen. Then he picks up the first bottle and places its neck under the stream of cold water. When it's full he places it to his right and as quickly as he can he reaches left and grabs another container, gets it under the flow of water in one smooth movement designed to keep as much water from spilling out onto the street as possible. He couldn't say why he does this. He just doesn't want to be responsible for waste. To him, water has come to mean life, and if more is to be lost, he doesn't want to be a part of it. He fills the second container with a practiced efficiency, and then the third, fourth, fifth, sixth.

Kenan has heard it said that you never hear the shell that kills you. He doesn't know if this is true, has no idea how anyone could know, or even pretend to know. When he hears the telltale whistle of an incoming shell, however, he knows that he has never heard this sound so close before. The shell is going to fall very near to him, and he can't accurately gauge where it's going to land because he has no experience in determining how this sound corresponds to proximity. In the split second before the shell hits he thinks of a time when he was a boy and got in a fight in the school yard. He wasn't much of a fighter, had never been in one before, and what he remembers is seeing the other boy's fist, seeing it coming at him slow like a yawn and thinking to himself, "I'm about to get punched in the face." Now, though, he sees that fist coming at him and thinks, "I'm about to die."

The shell hits, and an instant after hearing the loudest noise he thought the world could contain Kenan is knocked off his feet. The boy who punched him thirty years ago has grown into a prizefighter and punched him again. He sprawls on his back, and he stays down, dazed. His ears are ringing and he doesn't hear the whistle of the second incoming shell, but he hears its detonation. It echoes through his head for what feels like years, and then for a few seconds there is total silence. He wonders if he's gone deaf. His back is wet, and he assumes he's wounded, but as his hearing returns he hears screaming all around him, and he thinks that if he were wounded he would feel something.

Kenan finds he can't move. He wants to, but his limbs don't respond. Perhaps he's dead. He can see people running by him, down the street to the right, and he doesn't know why they're not stopping. Then he finds he can move his foot, and then his leg, and then his other leg and his arms, and he's restored to the land of the living. He sits up, feels himself for wounds, finds he's fine. He's sitting in a pool of water, though his bottles aren't tipped over. He isn't sure whether he should feel relieved or ashamed.

The shells hit about thirty meters up the street from him, near the end of the line. He stands and begins to walk toward where they landed. There are already people there, rushing, frantic, trying to save those who can be saved. On the pavement in front of him is a foot. The shoe is undamaged, as is some of the sock. It doesn't look real. Then he sees a woman holding her leg, stunned, as if she doesn't believe it either.

She looks at Kenan and begins to shriek, points at her leg to where her foot used to be. Two men rush toward her, one of them tying a piece of fabric around her leg at the thigh, and she passes out. The men pick her up and work their way up the street. There's a car waiting there, and they put her in the back, beside a man who has blood running down his face from a long gash in his head. His ear is attached to his head only at the lobe, but he doesn't seem to notice. The men close the door on the woman and move to the other side of the car to take a look at him. They confer and remove him from the car, placing him at the side of the road. He doesn't move, though his eyes are open, and Kenan realizes the man is dead.

Another group arrives with two more injured people, a man bleeding from his stomach and a child, maybe ten years old, who's unconscious. They're hastily placed in the car, the man in the back and the child in front. They remind Kenan of a family. In all likelihood they've never met before. He wonders what his own family is doing right now, is thankful that he hasn't brought any of his children with him, though they've asked time and time again, and he'd be glad for their company and the help carrying the water home. He can't risk one of them going home with another family.

One of the men bangs his hand on the rear window of the car and it speeds off. Kenan turns around, and in front of him is the man with the brown terrier. He's still holding the leash, or half of it. It's been severed, and the man's leg is bleeding. He looks at the space at the end of the leash, where his dog should be, then at the street around him.

"Have you seen my dog?" he asks Kenan.

"No," Kenan answers. "You're bleeding, sir."

The man doesn't seem to hear him. "Friend, have you seen my dog?"

Kenan puts his hand on the man's arm. "You're hurt. You need help."

The man ignores him, brushes off his hand. He limps away, stops a woman after a few steps, and repeats his question.

There are sirens in the distance, coming from the other side of the river, and then he hears the sound of shelling, followed by the sharp crack of sniper fire. They're firing at the ambulances sent to help, and as the sirens get closer he begins to worry that they're drawing the fire toward him, toward the brewery. But the men on the hills can hit the brewery anytime they like. They're firing at the ambulances to tell him, and everyone else, that help will not arrive if they have anything to say about it. Someone somewhere turns on the air-raid sirens, and the sound of the ambulances is drowned out. At the top of the street a car slides to a halt, and a few more people are deposited inside. The line of bodies on the side of the road has grown.

All around him people are screaming, running, shouting, moaning. Those who are injured but can walk are making their way to the top of the street in the hope that it won't be long before a car can take them. Kenan thinks they can hear the shelling as well as he can, so they must know their ordeal isn't over. Those who can't walk are being carried. The first of the ambulances arrives and unloads a half-dozen stretchers into waiting arms. The sound of the air-raid sirens swells and then dies off, swells again. After a while it begins to sound to him like the breathing of an asthmatic.

Kenan is able to identify three types of people here. There are those who ran away as soon as the shells fell, their instinct for self-preservation stronger than their sense of altruism or civic duty. Then there are those who didn't run, who are now covered in the blood of the wounded, and they work with a myopic urgency to help those who can be saved, and to remove those who can't to go to whatever awaits them next. Then there's the third type, the group Kenan falls into. They stand, mouths gaping, and watch as others run or help. He's surprised he didn't run, isn't part of the first group, and he wishes he were part of the second.

He looks down at his feet. He's only a few meters from where the first shell struck. There aren't many people left here now, no more than a dozen. In places the ground is stained dark red, but where he stands it's clean. Water runs down from the taps, which are undamaged, and there's a clear river in the center of the road. The gutter is turning pink, washing away the blood spilled only minutes ago.

Kenan walks back up the hill to his canisters. His six are full. He binds them together, three on each side. He looks at the water gushing out of the pipe in front of him. It won't be long before the street is clear again. He reaches out and puts his hands over the pipe. It's easy to block, and the water stops, but all around him other pipes continue to flow. He's soaked to the skin, and he knows that he can stand here with his hands on the pipe for a year and it will make no difference. He steps back, watches the water run downhill away from him. He imagines it traveling through the streets and ending up in the Miljacka, from there making its way out of Sarajevo until it runs into the ocean.

And this is how it goes. Buildings are eviscerated, burned, gutted, streetcars destroyed, roads and bridges blasted away, and you can see that, you can touch it and you can walk by it every day. But when people die they're removed, taken to hospitals and graveyards, and before the bodies are healed or cold the spot where they were shattered is unrecognizable as a place where anything out of the ordinary happened. This is why the men on the hills are able to kill with impunity. If there were bodies in the streets, rotting where they fell, if the water from these taps didn't wash away the blood and bone and skin, then maybe the men would be forced to stop, maybe they would want to stop.

At the top of the street an old Yugo hatchback takes away the last of the wounded. At the side of the road there are at least seven bodies. A large blue van pulls up. Four men get out and begin to put the corpses into the back, one man on each arm and one man on each leg. The bodies are loaded in feet-first, and as they're lifted into the van their heads loll back, as though taking one last look at the place where they died.

Kenan picks up one of Mrs. Ristovski's bottles. He pays no attention to the water that spills as his grip falters and the bottle tilts. When it's full he doesn't rush. He takes his time as he caps the first bottle, then fills the second one. He sets the bottles on the ground and stands there. He has grown used to the sound of the air-raid sirens, hasn't noticed it for a while. Now he hears them again, and he listens to them wail, listens to the screech of shells falling, the gunfire from both sides. He puts his hands back under the water, washes them even though they're not dirty, leans down, and puts the rope over his head. He picks up Mrs. Ristovski's water, one bottle in each hand, and stands. The rope cuts into his neck and shoulders, and he bends down, shifting it to a more comfortable position. Then he stands once more and turns away from the men who are loading the last of the bodies into their van. He begins to walk back down the hill, past the spot where the first mortar fell, then the spot where the second fell. He doesn't stop, doesn't look at the ground. There's nothing more to see.

At the bottom of the street Kenan stops. He isn't sure of his route. He can head to the east, cross at the library, using the same bridge he came over on, or he can go straight down-hill and take one of the two bridges that will be in his path. Both these routes are being shelled at the moment, and he's weighed down by the water, making it hard to run. He decides he has only two viable choices. He can find shelter and wait out the shelling, which could take hours, or he can cross at the Ćumurija Bridge, what little is left of it. Neither choice is appealing. The thought of waiting hours, possibly overnight, before crossing the Miljacka is too much, so he decides to cross the Ćumurija. It will mean carrying his load across bare steel girders, risking falling into the river. He'll have to make at least two, perhaps three trips to get all his water across. But it will be worth it to be home again, out of all this madness, wrapped back up in the temporary illusion of safety.

Kenan turns to his left, heads west. When he reaches the street leading north to one of the more direct bridges he looks down to the river and sees a car burning just before the deck of the bridge. It's the same model and color as the Yugo he saw at the brewery. He hopes it isn't the same one.

He takes a long breath, then another, and looks across the street. He picks out a reasonably sheltered doorway and tightens his grip on Mrs. Ristovski's bottles. He moves as fast as he can toward the doorway. When he's halfway across the street it occurs to him that he's waddling like a penguin and imagines what he must look like to anyone watching him. He remembers that the only person he needs to worry about watching him is one who's looking through a scope. Appearing like a penguin is the least of his worries. But then he wonders whether waddling like a fat, flightless bird makes him more or less likely to get shot. Do the men on the hills tend to shoot at people they find funny, or spare them? If he dressed in a penguin suit would he survive this war?

He reaches the doorway and stops for a rest. He's made it across without getting shot, but he'll never know whether it was because someone chose not to shoot him or if no one saw him at all. This bothers him, this lack of information, and then he realizes to his disgust that while he was crossing the street, while his life was in a gray space, he was making jokes to himself about penguins. There's no way that his friend Ismet sits in a hole on the front line and thinks such silly, meaningless thoughts. It's things like this that make him the coward he is, unable to help the wounded at a massacre, or a relatively un-harmed man searching for a dog. He didn't help the man look, or look himself, or even think about looking. He remembers the dog, a brown terrier, and he would know it if he saw it again. Perhaps it's still there. He should go back for it. It could be waiting in a doorway, or behind a pile of rubble, waiting for someone to find it.

But Kenan doesn't put down his water, doesn't go back to look for the dog. He has no doubt that the dog is dead, has always known it, and he knows that even if it wasn't, he wouldn't go back. Fear has paralyzed him as surely as a bullet to the spine, and he simply doesn't have what it takes to go back. Shame soaks through him. All he wants now is to go home and crawl into bed.

He leaves the doorway, continues westward. On his left is the abandoned army barracks, shelled to the ground by its former tenants. On his right is At-Mejdan, where slaves were sold, men were executed, and, later, horses raced. It's now a park, or it would be if there was still such a thing as a park in the city. Before the war he'd come here often with his family to hear outdoor concerts, and sometimes by himself to sit on a bench and drink a coffee on a warm fall day. He moves as quickly as he can, stopping every so often to catch his breath, but he doesn't linger any longer than he has to. He tries to keep his mind blank, to stop any thoughts that could render him motionless from prying their way into his mind.

As he doglegs to the north a group of bright green and yellow apartments comes into view, nicknamed "the parrots" by those in the city who thought they were an eyesore. Kenan himself never had a firm opinion about them, though he knew he wouldn't want to live there. Now, though, he's happy to see them, because they stand at the foot of the Ćumurija Bridge.

There's a man on the other side who has just begun crossing, and though it might be possible for two people to cross at once, if one of them stood aside in the middle and let the other pass, Kenan isn't sure whether he could balance with the water canisters, and he doesn't know whether this man would give him the right of way, so he decides to wait. He can't carry all the water over at once. Maybe he could if Mrs. Ristovski's bottles had handles and he could tie them in with his bottles, but with the way things are it's impossible. He decides he can take all his own bottles in one go, though. They're heavy but balanced, and if he takes three at a time there will be no way to balance them. He'll leave Mrs. Ristovski's bottles by some rocks and come back for them. Without his own bottles he'll be able to tuck one under his arm and hold the other in his hand, leaving one hand free to hold on to the side-rail of the bridge.

He thinks about this plan. He decides it's a good one, but is worried that someone will take Mrs. Ristovski's containers while he's crossing the bridge. He waits for the man on the bridge to finish crossing, nods hello to him as he passes, and then moves Mrs. Ristovski's bottles to a concealed spot, a small hole where the bridge meets the road. Satisfied that the bottles are safely out of sight, he shoulders his load of water and steps onto the bridge.

After a few steps he has to stop and steady the motion of his water jugs. They sway like pendulums, their momentum increased every time he steps forward. He slows their swing with his free hand, waits for them to hang motionless before moving forward again. He has to stop twice more before reaching the middle of the bridge. While he waits he looks to the east, and then back in the direction of the brewery. He tries to see if anything looks different from the way it did that morning, other than the still-smoking husk of the Yugo. Then it occurs to him that nothing should be different, because nothing has changed. Just because he was there this time, closer than normal to the epicenter of the slaughter, doesn't mean it's more relevant to the city. It's just another day.

The air-raid sirens have stopped. He thinks they've been stopped for a while, but he hadn't noticed. A shell falls somewhere far to the west, toward the airport. He takes a few steps, lets his load settle, takes a few more. His foot slips a little, which causes the canisters to sway forward, and on their backswing they hit him square in the knee, knocking him to the side. He hits the railing hard, is winded by the force of the blow. He holds on with both hands, puts his foot back on the girder beneath him, but he's shaken. He feels a rage wash over him, the way it does when he hits his head on the corner of a cupboard door or some object he didn't expect to be there, a rage that is focused and scattered all at once. He scrambles to the end of the bridge without stopping, adrenaline pushing him to it, and drops his water. He lies down on the ground, stomach pressed to the earth, not caring that he's out in the open, an easy target. He cries out, but doesn't recognize the sound that comes out of him. It's a baby and an animal and an air-raid siren and a man who has been knocked over by his own burden. He listens to it as it dissipates, gone like it never happened, and then he rolls over onto his back and looks at the sky.

He's tired. He's tired from getting water, and he's tired from the world he lives in, a world he never wanted and had no part in creating and wishes didn't exist. He's tired of carrying water for a woman who has never had a kind word to say to him, who acts as if she's doing him a favor, whose bottles don't have handles and who refuses to switch. If she likes the bottles so much, she should carry them to the brewery, she should watch as the street fills with blood and then washes itself clean, as a man stands with an empty leash and looks for a brown terrier while the dead are loaded into a van.

Kenan gets up off the ground. He looks back to the bridge, at the spot where he hid Mrs. Ristovski's water. He turns away, and picks up the rope binding his own bottles. His back bends into its yoke. The water rises into the air. Kenan takes a step and then another. Soon he will be home.

three

dragan

There's a small group of people around Emina, and they've removed her coat to get a better look at her arm. Someone hands it to Dragan, and he holds it, feeling useless. She's been shot just above the elbow, in the lower part of her biceps. It doesn't look life-threatening to Dragan, but someone has tied a tourniquet below her shoulder. A man who appears to know what he's doing says there's a major artery there that may have been severed. Dragan is skeptical, but then he remembers that when the doctor measures blood pressure the inflatable cuff goes around the same spot. Emina has lost a lot of blood, and is still bleeding, despite their efforts. The young man who saved her is gone. Dragan didn't see him leave, doesn't know which way he went.

There's an eruption of gunfire around Grbavica, possibly the defenders' answer to the sniper. If they know where he's firing from they might get him. Otherwise, it's probably a bluff, an attempt to make him think they know where he is. It could convince him to stop for a while. Or it could make him more determined. The volley of bullets might not even be connected with this particular sniper, or any sniper at all. It could even be the sound of the men on the hills trying to drive a wedge into the heart of the city. Dragan cannot decipher the sound of guns.

Someone has gone to flag down a car, or call an ambulance, Dragan can't remember which. It's unlikely that the phones work. The cars all travel so fast it's nearly impossible to get one to stop. Emina is still conscious, and doesn't seem to be in as much pain as he'd have expected. Her face is white.

He kneels beside her, and she half smiles when she sees him.

"You're still here," she says.

"Yes." He's ashamed, and wants to tell her so, but it's not for him to apologize. He hasn't earned the right.

"He's a better shot than we thought."

Dragan nods. "It's a good thing he's not better. You're lucky."

"I wanted to see the cellist play today. It's his last day. Jovan says he's finished after this."

A car races up the street, and a few of the group rush toward it and wave.

She sounds sleepy, her words slow and slurred. "Jovan will be upset. He doesn't like me going out. I just couldn't live as a prisoner. I had to get outside and walk around."

"Jovan will be fine," Dragan says. "And so will you." He

watches the approaching car. When he looks down at Emina her eyes are closed, but she's still breathing.

The car, dark red with four doors, stops. Its windshield is cracked, and the side of the car has several bullet holes in it. Two men rush out, leaving their doors open and the engine running. They take a quick look at the hatless man lying in the street, agree he's beyond help, and focus on Emina. After a cursory examination they pick her up and lay her in the backseat. They get back in the car and are moving before their doors are fully shut.

"Wait," Dragan calls. He wants to go with them, but they're already gone. He doesn't think they'd have let him come along, though, and he's not sure what he would have done at the hospital. The man who seems to know a bit about medicine stands beside him. "She'll be fine," he says. "Once she gets to the hospital they'll fix her up."

"It's not too bad?" Dragan asks, unsure whether the man is saying this because it's true or if he's trying to reassure him.

The man shrugs. "You can't have it much better and still be shot. It's a flesh wound."

Dragan looks at the man, believes him to be sincere. "Did you see it happen?"

"Yes. I was a few feet behind you."

Dragan nods and, after a long, uncomfortable silence, the man moves on, to the east, away from the intersection.

Dragan sits down on the cold concrete with his back against the boxcar. His hands still hold Emina's coat. Something in the pocket rattles, and when he reaches in he finds a bottle of pills and an address. It's these pills that brought Emina here today, her dead mother's blood thinners. He puts them in his own pocket, and then places the coat on the ground beside him. She won't want it now. No one wants the coat they were shot in, even if it were possible to wash out the blood and mend the holes. It was a nice coat when she wore it. Now it doesn't look like much to him. Just another piece of garbage.

His eyes move from the coat to the body in the street and back to the coat. Was being killed really better than being wounded? He isn't so sure now. The idea of knowing the moment of your death is imminent no longer seems so bad compared with an instantaneous ending. Emina will survive, of this he feels confident, but if she didn't, if she were more seriously wounded, wouldn't it be better to get one last look at the world, even a gray and spoiled vision, than to plunge without warning into darkness?

What makes the difference, he realizes, is whether you want to stay in the world you live in. Because while he will always be afraid of death, and nothing can change that, the question is whether your life is worth that fear. Do you face the terror that must come with knowing you're about to die for the sake of one last glimpse of life? Dragan is surprised to find his answer is yes.

A month ago, he was walking home from his shift at the bakery when a group of half-uniformed men surrounded him and, after examining his papers, ordered him to get into the back of a truck. They ignored his protests that his work at the bakery was deemed essential to the war effort by the government. They didn't care that he was sixty-four years old. He later found out they were the militia of one of the criminal bosses turned army commander, and they were paid according to how many men they rounded up.

There were seven other men in the back of the truck, and they were unloaded at the front lines, where they spent the next three days digging trenches. They had no weapons, and the only soldiers around were stationed behind them with orders to shoot if they abandoned their posts. They couldn't tell how close they were to the enemy, when they might be shot, where death would come from. It was difficult to guess how much time passed, and they were given no food. The only light was from the tracer bullets streaking through the sky, and the only sounds were the crunching of their shovels and the detonation of shells. The man next to him was so frightened he began to cry, and Dragan had to grab him by the shoulders and shake him to get him to stop, or at least to cry quietly. It was then that he decided it was better to be killed outright than to be wounded. The thought of spending his last hours in a hole he'd dug at gunpoint held no consolation when compared to his fear of death.

Later, after his superintendent at the bakery discovered where he was and contacted the necessary parties to secure his release, Dragan stopped distinguishing the streets of the city from those trenches, didn't care whether it was the men on the hills who were shooting or the defenders. It made no difference to him.

Now he wonders whether this was a mistake. He can see a very distinct difference between this street and the ditches he dug. A trench is used for war and only war. But on these streets, the streets of his city, he has walked with Raza's hand in his, and he has laughed with Davor. Today he shared a conversation with an old friend on one of his streets. There may be a war taking place on them as well, but they used to offer much more. This means something to him, although he can't put a name to it.

He knows he should have tried to help Emina. He should have rushed into the street with the young man and helped him to carry her. Perhaps that would have allowed them to go faster. But it's possible this would have made the sniper fire at them instead of at the man in the hat. There's no arguing with the outcome. Still, he didn't move when the shots were fired. Not because he thought anything through, but because he was afraid. If that makes him a coward, he's comfortable calling himself a coward. He isn't built for war. He doesn't want to be built for war.

Dragan looks east, toward his sister's apartment. He thinks of abandoning his trip to the bakery, of heading back. His brother-in-law isn't so bad. Maybe they could find something to talk about that would help bridge the gap between them. Perhaps they can have a coffee, if there's any left, if there's any water to brew it with or wood to heat it. He can always try to make it to the bakery again tomorrow, when he has a shift to show up for.

He doesn't want to go home, though. His head turns to the southwest, where, if he keeps on going past the bakery and then down through Mojmilo to Dobrinja, the not-so-secret tunnel leads under the airport into unoccupied territory.

He imagines himself handing a pass to an armed guard at the tunnel entrance. Where he could have gotten it he doesn't know, but no one gets by without a pass, and he imagines the guard inspecting his before allowing him through. He enters the tunnel, ducking low. The tunnel is poorly lit, and the air is stale. It takes him three-quarters of an hour to travel the 760 meters. The ground is covered in water in places, and he has to be careful not to trip over the rails that accommodate small carts. He's heard that some politicians and other important men sometimes ride in these carts, pushed by soldiers, but there's no one to push him. He doesn't mind, wouldn't accept an offer anyway. The tunnel passes under the foreign-controlled airport, where numerous people have been shot while trying to run across the tarmac. None of these people was able to secure permission to use the tunnel. The men on the hills picked them off like ducks on a pond.

As he nears the end of the tunnel the walls get wider and higher. He's able to stand up straight, and the air is a little fresher. When he emerges in the free territory of Butmir he's only eight kilometers from his sister's house. A fifteen-minute drive. But he's free. Two hours on a bus and he'll be on the coast. A ferry will deliver him to Italy. The whole trip will take less than a day. It's less than five hundred kilometers as the crow flies from Sarajevo to Rome. Not even an hour on an airplane. One and a half hours to Paris. Two hours to London. But he'll go to Italy, because that's where his wife and son are.

At first they won't believe he's there. Their mouths will hang open, and they will wonder if he's a ghost. He'll assure them he's not, of course, and then they'll be overcome with joy. Davor will hug him, his arms wrapped tight around his back, like he used to when he was a small boy. Raza will kiss him and run her hands through the hair on the back of his head. He'll take a shower, the water steaming hot, and dry himself with a soft, clean towel. They'll go out to a restaurant, and he'll eat whatever he likes, and he'll know that tomorrow he can do it all again. They'll walk through the streets, looking through the windows of shops. There will be trees, their leaves green, and the buildings will be bright and without scars. No one will be on the hills with guns pointed at them, and after a while he won't even think of this as a benefit, it will simply be an obvious thing, because that's how life is supposed to be. They will be happy. They won't hate anyone, and no one will hate them.

In the hills behind him a shell falls. He hears the rattle of automatic gunfire, and then another shell falls. It's a language, a conversation of violence. He's back in Sarajevo. There's no tunnel pass in his pocket, and there never will be. No one is getting out of town now. Certainly not him.

Dragan sits and listens to the men on the hills and the defenders in the city argue with projectiles. Nobody crosses the street. There are hardly any people even waiting, most having decided to take an alternative route, probably crossing the train tracks to the north and moving from east to west behind the protection of yet another barricade of railcars and concrete. Perhaps they're safer there, perhaps not. There's more than one sniper on the hills. They have enough men for every intersection if they choose.

He wonders what they think about, up there in the safety of their hills. Do they wish for this war to be over? Are they happy when they hit something, or is it enough to frighten people, to watch them run for their lives? Do they feel remorse when they go home and look at their children, or are they pleased, thinking they have done a great service for future generations? Dragan never understood, even before the war began, why they thought people like him were such a threat. He still doesn't understand what killing him would accomplish, what effect it would have on anyone but him.

Dragan doesn't want to go to Italy. He misses his wife and son, but he isn't Italian, and he never will be. There's no country he can go to where he won't be from Sarajevo. This is his home, and this is the city he wants to be in. He doesn't want to live under siege for the rest of this life, but to abandon the city to the men on the hills would mean that he would be forever homeless. As long as he's here, and as long as he can keep his fear of death from blinding him to what's left of the world he once loved and could love again, then there's still hope that one day he will be able to walk openly down the streets of this city with his wife and son, sit in a restaurant and eat a meal, browse the windows of shops, free from the men with guns.

Dragan knows he won't ever be able to forget what has happened here. If the war ends, if life goes back to some semblance of how it once was, and he survives, he won't be able to explain how any of it was possible. An explanation implies a logic, but there's no logic to Sarajevo now. He still can't believe it happened. He hopes he will never be able to.

arrow

The lightbulb in Nermin Filipović's office seems more oppressive than ever. Arrow would like nothing more than to reach up and swat it, send it flying into the ceiling. She resists the temptation, knows that the sound of the bulb breaking would bring an aide scurrying into the room to investigate. He would replace the bulb. It would accomplish nothing. It probably wouldn't even make her feel better.

She sits, alone, for nearly a half hour before Nermin arrives. He looks like he hasn't slept in days. He barely seems to notice her.

"It's done," she says as he falls into his chair.

"He's dead?" Nermin asks, looking at her for the first time.

Arrow nods. She's never seen him like this and doesn't know how to gauge his reactions.

"Which one?"

Arrow's face is blank. She doesn't understand the question.

"The cellist or the sniper?" he asks, leaning forward.

"The sniper," she says, her voice flat. She doesn't move, refuses to allow her body to reveal how she feels.

"Good." An assistant, a teenage boy who isn't old enough to shave, arrives in the room with a tray of coffee. Nermin takes one, hands the other to Arrow. She hesitates before accepting it, which prompts a look of surprise from Nermin. The boy retrieves his tray and leaves, shutting the door behind him.

Nermin takes a sip. "You seem unhappy."

Arrow says nothing. She drinks her coffee and keeps her eyes on the floor.

For a while neither of them speaks. Then, quietly, in a tone Arrow has never heard him use before, he says, "Maybe you have done this for long enough. Maybe you should stop now."

Arrow keeps her eyes on the floor. "The sniper had the shot. He had it the whole time. But he didn't shoot. He was listening to the cellist play."

Nermin shakes his head. "You don't understand me."

She continues. "I killed him because he shot at me, and because I couldn't trust him not to shoot later. I had no choice."

"No, you didn't. But this has nothing to do with the cellist. The time has come for you to disappear."

Arrow looks up. His bloodshot eyes stare at her. "Disappear?"

He wets his lips and looks away. "I can't protect you anymore. The terms of our deal can no longer be honored."

"I don't understand." Where, she wonders, am I to disappear to? The city is surrounded. No one can disappear, even if they want to.

"The men on the hills have created many monsters," he says, "and not all of them are on the hills. There are those here who believe they are in the right simply because they oppose something that is evil. They use this war and the city for their own ends, and I won't be a part of it. If this is how the city will be once the war is over, then it's not worth saving."

"What are they doing?" she asks. There are so many rumors these days that she doesn't know what to believe. Most of them are easily dismissed as propaganda, but some of them make her wonder.

Nermin takes a final sip of his coffee and sets the empty cup down on his desk. "You should disappear, now, so you don't have to find out." He stands, which in the past has been her signal to leave, but she doesn't move from her chair.

"What will happen to you?"

He steps out from behind the desk and stands beside her. "I expect to be relieved of my command at any moment."

Arrow stands, and when he leans in to kiss her on each cheek she hugs him. Despite remaining always at a distance, he has become the closest thing to a friend she has. She turns to leave, and he grabs her shoulder, says, to her back, "Your father would never have forgiven me for turning you into a soldier."

Arrow doesn't turn around. She places her hand on his. "My father is dead," she says, "and I forgive you."

As she walks out of his office and into the bright light of the street, her rifle feels heavier on her shoulder than ever before. She remembers what he said about the opposition of evil, and wonders whether she might believe the same thing herself. Does she think she is good because she kills bad men? Is she? Does it matter why she kills them? She knows she no longer kills them because they are killing her fellow citizens. That's just a part of it. She kills them because she hates them. Does the fact that she has good reason to hate them absolve her? A month ago she would have answered yes to this question. Now she wonders who decides what is a good reason and what isn't.

She doesn't know what will happen to Nermin. If he is right, if he is about to be relieved of his command, he will become a man without a place. The men on the hills will show him no mercy. Perhaps he has enough connections left to find a way to leave Sarajevo. It would be hard. Most countries won't accept anyone who's been a part of the fighting, and Nermin's high profile means that he won't be able to leave unnoticed. His best chance will be to stay out of sight until the war is over. If the men on the hills don't win, then perhaps things will change and he can reestablish himself in a time of peace. She's not sure exactly how a career soldier might do this, but lesser men have done greater things. She hopes that she is someday in a position to help him.

She has gone about three blocks when shelling starts. It's been a quiet day for the most part, but the sky is beginning to darken, and the men on the hills seem to have a fondness for marking the coming of night with shells. She's often wondered if the shells remind them of fireworks.

First they fall to the west, in Mojmilo and Dobrinja. Then a few land closer, across the river from Grbavica, and toward the riverbank around Baščaršija. Around her, people begin to move faster, heading home to the safety of cellars and basements, where they will likely spend the night. Arrow no longer goes into the basement of her building with the other residents when there's shelling. It doesn't seem worth it. Given that she's in more danger during her average day than she is during the worst night of shelling, she'd just as soon sleep in her own bed. If she's going to die, that's where she'd like it to happen. It's a small measure of control over an uncontrollable situation.

She's about to turn the corner and head north when a boy runs by her and clips her shoulder with his arm, almost knocking her over. He doesn't stop, but he glances back at her, and she recognizes him from Nermin's office, the one who brought coffee. He looks younger now. His face is frightened, almost white, and he's moving much faster than anyone else on the street. Several shells land on the hills above her, distracting her, and the boy is gone. She shakes her head. Why would Nermin have a boy on his staff who is so easily terrified? Then she stops walking. He wouldn't.

The boy isn't afraid of the shelling. Something is wrong. She turns around and heads back toward Nermin. Her mind is all static, a poorly tuned radio, and she's surprised to find herself running. The stock of her rifle bounces against her ribs, bruising them, and her boots feel as if they're full of water, sloppy and awkward. Though it's less than a minute, it seems to take days to travel a few blocks.

In a smooth and easy motion she slips her rifle off her shoulder and into her hands. Even as she's doing this she acknowledges that it is simply a reflex. It is unlikely her rifle can solve whatever is happening.

There is no time to ponder this insight, however, because a second after Nermin's office comes into view an explosion hurtles the doors off the building, sending the plywood covering the windows flying through the air. A ball of fire follows, blowing outward and then sucking back in on itself. The street is showered with dust and debris.

Arrow doesn't know if she was knocked off her feet by the explosion or if she went to the ground of her own volition. At first she doesn't even notice that she is on her stomach, watching the building burn through the scope of her rifle.

Nermin's office is on the ground floor of the three-storey

building. The rest of the building is also occupied by the military. Arrow doesn't know what goes on in the other rooms, but she knows right away that there wasn't anyone in them when the building exploded. Only one office would have had anyone in it.

The fire brigade arrives and puts out the fire. Men in uniforms block off the building and conduct a search. They don't find any survivors. It's lucky, they say, that the shell fell after work hours. A small miracle.

Arrow hears them talk to each other, can tell they all know it wasn't a shell that hit this building. No one wants to say it, or perhaps they're in on it. Either way, this explosion came from the inside and wasn't shell fire from the men on the hills. But no one says anything. After all, people are killed every day. Murder is commonplace. Why should this one be any different?

For several hours Arrow lingers, hoping that Nermin somehow escaped, that he had one more trick up his sleeve no one knew about. Then, after almost everyone has gone, two soldiers come out of the building carrying a body wrapped in a blanket. They load it into the back of a truck and drive off. She shoulders her rifle and turns away from the building, begins the long walk home.

The bombarding hasn't let up at all. The men on the hills are having a busy night. Arrow lies in her bed, listens to the sound of shells falling, of automatic gunfire, of sirens. She wonders what will be left standing when morning comes, whether there will be any noticeable difference in the appearance of the city. There must come a point where so much has been turned to rubble that ruining a little more makes no difference. It's possible that point has already been reached.

Does a person work the same way? She can't tell. It seems that she should be more upset about Nermin's death, or more angry, or more anything. She wants to be, but she isn't. She can't even claim to be surprised.

It's cold tonight, and the electricity is still off. She has no more firewood for her improvised woodstove, hasn't bothered to scrounge for any. She shivers under her blankets, gets up and goes to the hall closet for more, returns to bed and continues to shiver. Her stomach grumbles, protesting her small supper of rice and weak tea. She can't stand rice. She doesn't remember disliking it before the war, but now the very thought of rice revolts her. It's all she has, though, all that's left from the last round of humanitarian aid. She gets paid in cigarettes by the army, which she trades for small things like a square of chocolate or a bar of soap. She managed to get a bag of apples a few weeks ago and even though they were soft and mealy, they were well worth the ridiculous price she paid in a moment of weakness. She still has cigarettes to trade, a drawer full of them, but she can't be bothered. It seems a waste to her, somehow, and she can't shake the feeling that she may need them later on. So she eats rice, works her way through the ten-kilogram sack in the corner of the kitchen, augmenting it with bread and weak tea.

"Disappear," Nermin told her. He's right, she should disappear. Her stash of cigarettes might be enough to buy a pass through the tunnel. She has no idea what that costs. But she can't stop thinking about Slavko's funeral, the fat man, and the grave. Is there a difference between disappearing and going into a grave? Does it matter whether she succumbs to the wishes of the men on the hills or the men in the city?

There is, of course, the question of survival. She doesn't want to die. She doesn't want to be shot by anyone, regardless of whether they're on the hills or in the city. But the young girl who was overcome by what it means to be alive, the girl who was so happy and afraid and awestruck that she had to pull her car to the side of the road, doesn't want to die either. That girl may be gone for now, may have no place in the city of today, but Arrow believes it's possible that someday she might return. And if Arrow disappears, she knows she's killing that girl. She will not come back.

Then there is the cellist. A part of her job is done. She has killed the sniper they sent. But if the cellist is true to his pledge, and Arrow believes he will be, then he is not yet finished. So they may send another sniper. They will have trouble finding a willing man, knowing what happened to his predecessor, but it is possible they will try again. And where will she be if that happens? Will she be protecting the cellist? She wants to protect him. If it is in her power, she will.

Arrow wakes to the sound of boots in the stairway. She doesn't remember falling asleep and feels as though she hasn't. But her eyes open, and she knows that the boots she hears are not on the feet of any of her neighbors. There is a pounding at the door. She gets out of bed, pulls on her clothes, and opens the drawer to the small table beside her bed. She takes out her father's revolver, the gun he used during his time as a police officer, and puts it in the pocket of her coat. Her rifle sits on the table in the kitchen, clean and ready, but she leaves it where it is.

Whoever is there continues hammering away, and she hears her neighbor's door open. There is a pause, during which no words are spoken, and then the neighbor's door closes again. Arrow checks that her gun is loaded, then answers the door.

Three men wait on the other side. One of them has his fist raised, ready to strike the door again, and the other two stand further back from him. They carry guns, appearing casual. She knows they are anything but. They all wear hiking boots. The one who's knocking is wearing green fatigues and an army jacket with a patch bearing the country's insignia sewn on it. The other two wear street clothes, with no identifying badges on them at all.

The man in green looks at her in a way that reminds her of the way men used to look at her in nightclubs. He pauses before speaking, looking at the other two. "Are you Arrow?" His voice is intended to sound tough, but comes across as almost comic.

"Possibly. What do you want?" Her hand is in her coat pocket, but she hasn't decided what to do yet. She could kill all three of them before they even raised their weapons, but that doesn't seem like the correct course of action. They don't appear to pose an immediate threat to her. They're more likely messengers. Don't shoot the messenger, the old saying goes, though she can't remember exactly why. She decides to make no move for now.

"Come with us."

Arrow pauses, wonders what her choices are. Does a refusal mean she must kill these men? "I don't think so," she says.

The two at the rear move their hands on their guns to a less casual position, raise the barrels slightly, and Arrow gets the answer to her question.

"This is not a request," the one in front says, though she can see it is. He is jumpy, she thinks. These men have heard of her. They might not be sure if the stories they've heard are true, but they've heard enough to be afraid. She feels pleased, momentarily, and then is irritated with herself for reveling in the fear of others. She never wanted anyone to fear her.

"Where are we going?" she asks, her voice low and smooth. She wants them to know they do not intimidate her.

"To see Colonel Karaman," he says. "Bring your rifle."

Arrow waits, lets them sweat it out while she decides what she'll do. She can say no, and she will have to kill these three men, which will result in her being a fugitive. It seems easier and more prudent to go with them. She has never heard of a Colonel Karaman, and that makes her nervous. She nods and walks away from them, into the kitchen. She picks up her rifle and returns to the door. She closes the door, and the three men fall into step with her, the one in jeans beside her and the other two behind. She gets the distinct feeling they are treating her as a prisoner.

Arrow steps out of a blue BMW and is directed to wait while one of the men goes inside a café in a narrow street just north of the library. The other two men stand nearby, smoking, but they don't try to talk to her. After a few minutes the first man returns and motions for her to follow him.

The inside of the café is poorly lit, and the air is stale. The windows have been barricaded with sandbags, and there is very little furniture left in the room. At a table in the back corner sits a man in uniform. He is in his late forties, and his hair and beard are graying. His face is tanned, his eyes an indistinguishable shade of brown. He looks hard, a man used to fighting. Arrow is immediately aware that he'd make a dangerous enemy.

"Sit," he says, pushing out a chair with one of his feet. "And leave your rifle by the door."

Arrow sets her rifle down, gently, and sits. She feels uneasy, aware that the situation is getting out of hand. She waits for the man to speak, eager to try to find a way to regain some control over what will happen.

"My name is Colonel Edin Karaman," the man says, his voice curt. "You are known as Arrow?"

"Yes."

"And what is your real name?"

He looks at her, expecting an answer. Arrow straightens her spine and looks back at him. "Arrow is as real a name as I have," she says.

He pauses. "It doesn't matter," he says. "If I needed to know your name I'd already know it." He takes a file from some papers sitting on the table, opens it, and lights a cigarette. "Your unit has been disbanded. You have been reassigned to me."

He doesn't look at her as he says this, but Arrow is aware that he is gauging her reactions. "What about Nermin Filipović?"

"Filipović has been killed, as you are aware." He looks up. "I have been watching you for some time. You possess an impressive range of abilities."

Arrow looks at Edin Karaman's hands. They are smooth, clean, and have no calluses. They are at odds with the rest of him. "What do you want from me?"

"I want you to continue what you have been doing," he says, closing the file. "But under my direction."

"No," Arrow says, "that's not how I work."

He smiles. "You misunderstand."

Arrow shakes her head. "I don't think I do."

"Yes," he says, "you are very much mistaken. I am not asking you. I am ordering you. We are at war. I didn't ask for this war, but they insisted, and now they must bear the results. You are a part of the solution, and will act as such."

"I have an assignment already," she says, "which I must finish." She is sweating, feels a drop trickle down the back of her calf.

"The cellist is no longer your concern. We have assigned someone else to him." He inhales a deep drag of his cigarette.

"Why?"

"Because I say so. Filipović has misused your talents, allowed you to be wasted on ordinary soldiers and irrelevant endeavors like this cellist business." Edin Karaman stands. "You will go with the men outside. They will take you to meet your spotter. He will give you the details of your first assignment."

Arrow doesn't get up. She places her hands on the table and stares up at him. "I don't work with a spotter. I choose my own targets."

He looks down at her. "No, you don't. Again I remind you that you are not being presented with a choice here. You will do what is required to defend this city, as decided by me. Now go."

She hesitates, unsure of what to do. She has been naive and has lost control over herself. She is entirely without options.

As she rises to her feet and turns to leave, she wonders what her father would say to her if he were alive. Did he know this would happen? Did he understand better than she realized the mechanics of a war and the people who operate on each side in a war? She doubts it. He was just a father wanting his daughter to be safe. He couldn't have known that she would be so good at killing, or that this skill would make her vulnerable.

"One last thing," he calls. She turns to face him. His face is severe, his hands folded in front of him. "Some in this city like to think that this war is more complicated than it really is. In case you are one of these people, I will tell you the reality of Sarajevo. There is us, and there is them. Everyone, and I mean everyone, falls into one of these two groups. I hope you know where you stand." He unfolds his hands and waves her away, the way one would shoo a fly off a dinner plate.

Arrow bends down and picks up her rifle. Its familiar

weight comforts her. If they want her to kill the men on the hills, then fine, she will kill the men on the hills. Whatever has happened in her life, the choices she has already made, they have led her to this point. All that remains are the consequences.

kenan

Kenan moves at a determined pace through town, over the eastbound tram tracks, north through Strossmayer Street, and over the westbound tram tracks. As he reaches the other side of the main road he stops for a rest, lets his bottles sink to the ground. As he prepares to lift them again he sees Ismet coming down the hill, and he waits as his friend approaches.

Ismet smiles when he sees him. "What took you so long?"

Kenan doesn't smile back. He isn't sure what to say. "There was shelling at the brewery."

Ismet nods, his face turned grim. "Are you okay?" he asks, looking him over.

"I'm fine. Where are you going?" He knows that Ismet can tell he's not fine, but he doesn't want to talk about it now.

"The market. Come with me," he says, moving to pick up Kenan's water.

"Are you out of centipedes already?" Kenan heaves the water up before Ismet can take it.

"Let me help you, at least."

"It's fine. There's no way to balance it if you help. Really." He turns west, toward the market. "Let's go." He has fifteen marks in his pocket. If he's lucky, he might be able to find something that's a deal. Something for the children, perhaps.

As they walk toward the market, he notices that Ismet isn't smoking. Normally he would, he thinks, and a part of him wishes Ismet would offer him another cigarette. He wonders if he is the reason Ismet isn't smoking, if he feels obliged to share.

The market is crowded, and Kenan is made bulky by his water. "Wait here," Ismet says, "and I'll see if there's anything worth buying. I'll come get you if there is."

He watches Ismet disappear into the throng. This is one of the city's busiest outdoor markets, but it's not a large space, and they've crammed as many tables into the square as they can. It's not the real black market, this place, though it's certain that many of the items for sale have entered the city through illicit means. He's been shopping here for most of his life and a good percentage of the food that he's eaten, the food that has built him into the person who stands here now, has come from these tables. He never imagined it could feel as though this market were holding him hostage.

Kenan thinks about the tunnel, how it could be used to get all the children out of Sarajevo, how it could be used as a way to save the city. Instead, it's lined with rails to carry cars that bring in the goods being sold here at their ridiculously inflated prices. It's the new tram. And then Kenan understands what happened to his washing machine. He hadn't thought about it at the time, but what would anyone want with an electrical appliance in a city that didn't have electricity? He sees, now, that the railcars that enter Sarajevo laden with goods bound for the black market do not leave empty. Somewhere, in a city other than this hell, someone is washing their clothes in a machine they purchased for a song, knowing or not knowing that they are accomplices in the destruction of his city.

Up the street, to the west, he sees a man standing beside a black Mercedes. He's dressed in a brand-new tracksuit, and he is clearly well fed. He stands, smoking, seeming to be waiting for something. Every so often he looks up the street, toward Kenan, in the direction traffic comes from.

A large truck drives by. Kenan recognizes it from the brewery, one of the trucks used to haul water that sped by him on his way up the hill. He assumed it was bound for the troops at the front lines or the hospital. But the truck stops behind the black Mercedes, and the driver gets out and talks to the man standing beside it. He can't tell what they're saying, but the man hands the driver a piece of paper and slaps him on the back. The driver gets back into the truck, pulls out into the street, and disappears down the road. Kenan has no idea where he's going, but he understands completely what he's just seen, knows that the water in that truck isn't bound for anyone who deserves it.

At first he just stands there, shocked. But as it sinks in, he begins to understand. Of course they buy and sell water. They buy and sell everything else, why should this be different? If he had money himself, he would pay whatever it cost to take this day back, not to have seen and done what he has. But it isn't right, all the same. They should not be able to do this.

And now he is angry. All he sees is the man in the tracksuit beside the Mercedes, and all he wants to do is put his hands around his throat. He takes a step forward, feels the rope that holds his water fall from his shoulders. He stops, takes another step, stops again. He can't afford to leave the water. It would be gone before he even got to the man in the tracksuit.

Kenan goes back, retrieves the fallen rope. He heaves up the water, its weight now a familiar burden. It seems unlikely to him that he will ever be free of it. So be it. He'll carry this water on his back forever, like Atlas and his world, and that is fine. He lurches forward, his vision tunneling into the man in the tracksuit.

The man is smoking a cigarette, looking back toward the marketplace. His movement is languid. He's not in any particular hurry. He turns, looks in Kenan's direction. He looks right at him, seems to laugh at the sight of him trying to run while carrying all this water. The man doesn't know that Kenan is coming for him, that he is the reason for the comical sight he smiles at. This only makes Kenan angrier.

The man in the tracksuit flicks his cigarette onto the ground, walks around to the other side of his car, and opens the door. He digs around in his pockets until he finds a pair of sunglasses. He breathes on the lenses, wipes them on the T-shirt he wears under his tracksuit, and gets into the car. The Mercedes rumbles to life and accelerates into the street. By the time it disappears from view, Kenan is only three-quarters of the way to where the man was standing.

Kenan continues on. He stops where the Mercedes was parked, looks down at the man's discarded cigarette. It still smokes, unfinished, a good amount of tobacco remaining. It's an American cigarette, the kind Kenan never really liked but would smoke if he had to. He hasn't had one of these since the war started.

An old woman scuttles past him, bends down and picks up the cigarette. With a shriveled hand she drops it into a tin can and continues down the street, never glancing up. She looks more like a crab than a person.

He hears music. It's faint, and the sound comes and goes, sometimes drowned out by the noise of the street, but in the quieter moments it returns. Without knowing why, without feeling he has to have a reason, Kenan follows the sound across the street, back into town. After a short block the music grows louder, and he sees a small crowd of people standing tight up against the buildings lining the south end of the street. They are all looking at something, he can't tell what.

He turns the corner and sees what it is they're looking at.

He finds a spot against a wall, sets down his water bottles, and joins them.

Kenan knows this man. He's seen him play before, though he can't remember where. His tuxedo is dirty and his shoes are scuffed. His hair is black and matted, his beard a patchy accessory to a thick, long mustache. There are large, dark circles under his eyes. The man looks like he's been in a fight, and he looks like he's lost.

Kenan has heard of this. Someone, maybe Ismet, maybe his wife, has told him that a cellist was playing every day in the street where the people were killed while lining up for bread. It was a week or so ago. The cellist saw the whole thing happen, watched it from his window. When Kenan was told of what the cellist was doing, he didn't say anything but thought it was a bit silly, a bit maudlin. What could the man possibly hope to accomplish by playing music in the street? It wouldn't bring anyone back from the dead, wouldn't feed anyone, wouldn't replace one brick. It was a foolish gesture, he thought, a pointless exercise in futility.

None of this matters to Kenan anymore. He stares at the cellist, and feels himself relax as the music seeps into him. He watches as the cellist's hair smoothes itself out, his beard disappears. A dirty tuxedo becomes clean, shoes polished bright as mirrors. Kenan hasn't heard the cellist's tune before, but he knows it anyway, its notes familiar and full of pride, a young boy in a new coat holding his father's hand as he walks down a winter street.

The building behind the cellist repairs itself. The scars of bullets and shrapnel are covered by plaster and paint, and windows reassemble, clarify, and sparkle as the sun reflects off glass. The cobblestones of the road set themselves straight. Around him people stand up taller, their faces put on weight and color. Clothes gain lost thread, brighten, smooth out their wrinkles.

Kenan watches as his city heals itself around him. The cellist continues to play, and Kenan knows what he will do now. He will walk up the street to his apartment. He'll take the stairs two at a time, not even breathing fast, and throw open his door. Amila will be surprised to see him, and he'll grab her and kiss her, like he used to when they were much younger. He'll run his fingers through her hair, thick and the color of honey.

Their son, Mak, will walk into the room, wondering what the commotion is. "Gross," he'll say when he sees them, and Amila will pull away from him laughing.

Together they'll all walk down into the city. He'll hold his younger daughter's hand. "Daddy," she'll say, "can we get ice cream?"

Kenan will smile and say yes, and Sanja will squeeze his hand tighter, excited. His oldest, Aida, will pout a little at first, concerned that she may miss her plans to see a movie with her boyfriend, whom Kenan is still not sure he likes, but it won't take long for her to soften up. She has never been able to stay mad for very long, just like her mother.

They will tramp through the city, through Baščaršija, down past the library, where there is a concert taking place under the glass dome of the main hall. At a small restaurant just west of the library, which he's been going to since he was a boy, they'll eat until their stomachs can hold no more. He will have lamb stew and *ćevapi*, and laugh with the waiter when he spills a coffee on the table, their hands darting out to save their food and stop the hot liquid from running onto their laps. On the way home they will stop and Sanja will get her ice cream, and, though Kenan can tell she's full, she'll insist on finishing the whole thing, which will make Amila worry a little.

They'll be tired, full, and slightly sleepy, so they'll take the tram to the foot of their street instead of walking back, and Kenan will stand holding on to the rail while his family sits. The city will slide by him like water in the Miljacka, its streets full of people, normal, happy people worried only about whether it might rain tomorrow.

They'll get off the tram, and Kenan will watch until it curves out of sight, heading west toward the airport. Tomorrow he'll catch it bright and early, be at work before anyone. Chelsea lost today, and he'll give Goran a hard time, ask him why he can't cheer for a proper team.

He will hug his daughter, Aida, who is off to her movie. "Be careful," he'll tell her. "Teenage boys are nothing but trouble." She'll roll her eyes at this, but then she'll lean in and kiss him on the cheek.

"I know, Dad," she'll say, and he'll press some money into her hand.

"Buy your own popcorn. That way you're not beholden."

She'll roll her eyes at him again, but she's not mad, and he'll stand with his arm around Amila and watch as she crosses the street, hurrying, not wanting to be late. Kenan will look at his wife, and then his son and younger daughter, and he will know how happy he is, and none of this will ever be taken away from him.

But it is all taken away. The music is over, the notes stop. He is back on the street where twenty-two people were killed while waiting to buy bread. Maybe a blue van took their bodies away. Maybe their heads lolled back as they were loaded in, giving them one final look at the street where they were killed.

The cellist rests his hands, opens his eyes. He doesn't acknowledge the small crowd, and they don't applaud. A few people have laid flowers at his feet, but they are not for him. Kenan wishes he had something to leave, but all he has is water and fifteen German marks. The flowers on the ground are beyond watering. Nothing he has will make the least bit of difference.

The cellist stands, picks up his stool, and turns away from the street, enters a doorway, is gone. Kenan wonders for a moment if he was ever there. The crowd of people disperses, a few at a time, until there is just Kenan and one old woman. She stands looking at the pile of flowers and the blast mark on the pavement where the mortar landed.

She turns to Kenan. "My daughter," she says, "she was here to buy bread."

Kenan isn't sure why the old woman is telling him this.

"She didn't need any, but I asked her to see if she could get me some." The woman's voice is soft, calm. It seems to him that her tone doesn't fit with what she's telling him.

He tries to think of something he can say that will mean something, that will bring her comfort or hope or anything positive, but he can't. He nods at her, feels his chest tighten.

"What should I tell my grandchildren when they ask how their mother died?" She turns away, and Kenan understands that she does not expect an answer to her question. He has none to give her. They stand, silent, and look at the street and the flowers. A shell falls, behind them, somewhere on the left bank of the river, but neither flinches. After a while, the old woman moves to leave.

"Did your daughter like the cello?" Kenan asks, surprising himself. He doesn't know why he's asked this, isn't sure why it matters. The woman stops, and he's afraid he's made things worse, spoken out of turn.

"I don't know," she says. "She never said so to me."

"I think she was a great lover of music," he says, and he does think this, is sure of it.

The old woman turns, looks at him, but he can't tell what's in her mind. She exhales a long, slow breath, smiles a small smile. She nods twice, turns, and continues down the street.

Kenan stays a while longer, then picks up his water and goes back to the market. As he's about to cross the street he sees Ismet. He's bartering with a man, hands waving wildly, striking the air. The man doesn't relent, or at least he doesn't appear to. Ismet's hands sink, his shoulders slump a little, and, shaking his head, he reaches into his pocket and pulls out three packs of cigarettes. He places them on the table, and the man hands him some bills.

Kenan watches as Ismet takes the bills to a table in the middle of the market, where he trades them with a woman for a small bag of rice. It's what the world sent them, relief, and though it's not supposed to be sold, it is. Kenan knows that Ismet risked his life for those cigarettes, got them as a substitute for pay from the army. Now he's watched his friend trade them for something that he should have been given for free in the first place, but wasn't, so greasy men in tracksuits and greasy men in business suits can get rich.

There is the sound of shooting coming from Grbavica, and every so often he hears shelling on the left bank, and also to the west, near the airport. The men on the hills are busy today.

Their business is brisk, and they will have a lot of customers. He thinks about the woman whose daughter was killed in the bread line, wonders how many women there are like her in the city, how many people walk the streets as ghosts. It must be a lot. They can fill up every spare scrap of land with graves, they can turn every park and football field and yard into a graveyard, and that will still not account for the dead. There are dead among the living, and they will be here long after this madness ends, if it ever ends.

He thinks of Mrs. Ristovski. He doesn't know what made her the way she is, but something has killed her, he can see now that she is a ghost as well. She has been a ghost for a long time. And to be a ghost while you're still alive is the worst thing he can imagine. Because, like it or not, sooner or later we all become ghosts, we are washed away from the ground until even the memory of us is gone. But there's a time when we are not, and you have to know the difference. Once you forget, then you are a ghost.

Kenan will not be a ghost. Enough has been done to this city in the name of ghosts. He tells himself this, as though saying it will make it true. You are not a ghost. You are not a ghost. But as he repeats these words, he knows that saying them will not make them true. All the words in the world cannot keep him from fading away.

He sees Ismet coming out of the market, walking to the spot where he left Kenan. Kenan picks up his water, moves away from the market. Ismet won't find him waiting, but he'll probably figure he got tired and took his water home. He'll see him later on. They'll share a joke, talk about their families, hope for this to be over. They will be the ones who rebuild Sarajevo, when the time comes. They will put every brick back, replace every window, patch every hole. They will rebuild the city without knowing whether this is the last time it will be done. They will earn the right to do this, any way they can, and when it is done they'll rest.

Kenan turns south, away from home. In a few hours it will be dark, but he'll be home long before then. He begins to work his way toward the Ćumurija Bridge, where two bottles of water without handles wait for him in a small hole.

They take her to what's left of the Parliament Building, one of the tallest buildings in town. The men on the hills have hit it with hundreds of shells, set it on fire, then fired hundreds more shells at it. The tower is a target not only because it is a symbol of a government they have vowed to destroy but also because all of Grbavica is visible from its upper floors.

Arrow has always avoided this building, partly because it's an obvious place for a defender to operate out of, making it the subject of frequent attacks, and partly because it's full of other members of her own army. She's considered it ground already claimed.

In the lobby, which is surprisingly undamaged, a man is waiting for her. He stands by the elevators, smoking. There are two guards stationed at the entrance, but they pay her and her escorts little attention. She walks across the marble floor, past two large green potted plants.

"The higher floors are worse," the man waiting says to her, as though reading her mind.

The three men who have been attached to her like snails to a leaf since this morning nod at the man, satisfied that they have fulfilled whatever job they were given, and leave.

"Not the sharpest knives, those three," the man says after they've gone. He's about her age, no more than thirty. He's tall, has the sort of face that looks amused regardless of the situation, and curly hair. He's wearing a pair of gray coveralls and holds a semiautomatic rifle in his hand. "I'm Hasan," he says.

"Arrow," she says. She tries not to be taken in by this man's friendliness.

"Of course. I've heard of you. I didn't think you existed." He's smiling, and she can't tell whether he's being serious or not.

"I don't know what you've heard," she says, "but it's probably not true."

"Probably not," he agrees. "Still, it'll be nice for a change to work with someone who knows what they're doing."

He puts out his cigarette and opens a door leading to a staircase. "How does fourteen strike you?"

"Fine," she says.

They walk up fourteen flights in silence. The stairwell is dark, the only light available coming from a small flashlight Hasan holds out in front of him. She can smell smoke. She loses count of their progress, and when they reach their floor she accidentally bumps into him when he stops to open the door.

"Sorry," she says.

"No problem." He turns off his flashlight and puts it back into his pocket as they step out of the stairwell.

Hasan wasn't joking when he said the upper floors were worse. What isn't burned has been splintered by shells. There's broken glass, twisted metal, and other unrecognizable debris strewn across the rooms, and the wind blows freely through the missing windows and gaping holes in the outer walls.

"Are you ready to go hunting?" he asks, his voice low, no longer as carefree.

"No," she says, "I'm not."

Hasan steps back, looks at her. "I don't understand."

"What, precisely, are we doing here?" She asks the question a little louder than she intends to.

"This is an easy one. Colonel Karaman probably just wants to make sure you're as good as they say before giving you anything more difficult. We're going to move into position, I'm going to select a target, and you'll fire. Easy. You'll do fine." He looks at her expectantly.

"Who are we shooting?"

Hasan shrugs. "I haven't decided yet. One of them. We'll see who's available."

Arrow wonders how she's ended up here, what she has done to box herself into this corner. She can't think of anything specific, and this irritates her.

"This way," Hasan says, and he leads her up the corridor

toward the southern end of the building. When they are about five meters from the windows he signals for her to get down, and from there they crawl on their stomachs. They reach the outer wall, and he points up at the windows, begins to get to his feet. The windows are a meter off the ground, and offer no real cover from view. To get a shot she'd have to stand and fire, making her a target for anyone with a rifle in either Grbavica or the hills above.

"No," Arrow says. "There." She points at a hole in the wall, about thirty centimeters wide. For a second she thinks Hasan will refuse, but he agrees, and they crawl to the hole. She positions herself, and Hasan puts down his gun and takes a pair of binoculars out of his coveralls. He raises himself up to the window, takes a quick look around, and sinks back down.

"This is a good spot," he says.

Arrow looks through her scope. Grbavica is a wasteland. She can't find a single structure that doesn't bear the mark of weapons. The streets are barely streets anymore. The pavement is torn apart, littered with mangled cars and pieces of buildings. She sees a few people, but no soldiers. They've learned the sight lines of this building and know not to wander into them. She wonders how they're going to find anyone to shoot.

"I used to live there," Hasan says. "You see that red building, about a hundred meters west of the bridge?"

She sees it. It's on the front lines, badly damaged. It would have been a nice place to live before the war, though. Right on the river, lots of trees.

"I was at work when the men on the hills came in their tanks and took over. If I hadn't been, I'd be dead now. They killed my younger brother. He was twelve. My father as well. I don't know where my mother and sisters are. All I've been able to find out is that they're not in Grbavica anymore."

Arrow doesn't know what to say. His story is not uncommon. She's not sure if he expects her to say anything. She hopes not.

"They're probably dead too. I almost hope they are. Better that than have them forced to live with those monsters." He says this without emotion, with a matter-of-fact frankness that startles her.

"My father was killed too," she says, surprising herself. "In the first battle at the Canton Building."

Hasan nods. "We will make them pay for what they've done, to us, to everyone."

Arrow doesn't reply, but an uneasy feeling is setting in. There's something about the tone of Hasan's desire for vengeance that unnerves her. She has felt this desire for retribution herself many times, has killed because of it. She can't work out why it's bothering her now.

Hasan returns his attention to the window. Arrow looks through her scope, scanning the streets for anything that looks military. It can sometimes be difficult to tell who is a soldier and who isn't. The men on the hills are mostly an irregular force, and they usually don't wear uniforms. If they have a gun, they're obviously combatants, but many of them don't always have their weapons visible or, in the case of officers or other senior-ranking officials, don't carry anything other than handguns, which are hard to spot from a distance. She's found that a lot can be detected from the way a person moves, how the other people around him move. An officer walks with a swagger, and those around defer to him, move out of his way. Soldiers tend to travel in groups, with the lowest-ranking one leading the way. Patience is rewarded, often, by letting one man go by without shooting. Others usually follow. Choosing a target can be a real art. She wonders how Hasan will go about it, and whether he will choose well.

She knows she's rationalizing, and that a principle has been compromised, but she has little choice. And all in all, she can't argue that these men with guns haven't earned the bullet that will find them. If she is the one to deliver it to them, well, that is how it will be. She made her choice months ago. It's fortunate, she supposes, that she was able to go for so long without becoming part of the larger machinery of her army.

"There," Hasan says. "I've found one."

"Where?" she asks. She can't see anything worth shooting at.

"Two o'clock, fifty meters south of the yellow bus."

Arrow looks, and just past a burned-out bus a man is walking up the hill. He's trying to stay close to the buildings, but he's miscalculated the line of sight and is in easy range. But something's wrong about him. He's old, probably in his early sixties, and his clothes are too worn for him to be a soldier. There's no confidence in his walk, no authority, and he's clearly unarmed.

"That man's a civilian," she says. "He's no soldier."

"He's our target," Hasan says. "I pick who to shoot at, not you."

"No," she says. "He's no good." She searches for another target. Up the road from the old man she sees a small glint, a momentary shine of metal, and then a man takes a step to the right, into her line of fire. He moves like a soldier, is smoking a cigarette. He shifts his weight, and his rifle becomes visible. It's apparent he's unaware of his vulnerability, has become lazy and inattentive. He's talking to someone she can't see, so he's not alone.

"There, to the south. There's a soldier." Her finger brushes the trigger. She will give Hasan the courtesy of giving the order, but her mind is already made up.

"No," Hasan says. "Forget him. I've made the choice. Fire at my target."

Arrow takes her finger off the trigger, looks up at Hasan. "I'm not going to kill an unarmed civilian."

Hasan turns to her. "You'll kill who I tell you to kill."

Arrow shakes her head. "No."

Hasan slides down from the window. "What do you think this is, some sort of game?"

"I could ask you the same thing," she says.

"Fire your weapon."

"No. I'll kill the soldier."

Hasan looks at her, shakes his head. "We're not negotiating here. Other people can shoot the soldiers. That's not our job."

Arrow takes her hands off her rifle, turns to get a better view of Hasan. "What do you mean?"

"I mean you're not an ordinary soldier. Colonel Karaman's unit is not just any unit."

"You kill civilians?"

He laughs. "Sure. We do a lot of things. This is merely a test, one you are failing. You think that man's an innocent? Answer me this. How is it he's able to walk the streets in Grbavica freely? Why isn't he dead, or in a camp, or whatever else they do?"

Arrow knows the answer to this, knows it is because the men on the hills view him as one of their own. "That doesn't mean he's one of the men killing us."

"It doesn't matter. He's one of them. They are his sons, he is their father, or grandfather, or uncle. They have killed our fathers and grandfathers and uncles."

"We're better than this."

"Of course we are. They're rabid animals. Killing them does the world a favor."

Arrow thinks about this, wonders how many of the men on the hills she has killed. Their deaths saved lives. She knows this is true. And she knows that she has nothing but contempt for the ones who murder. But they're not all like that. Their mothers and fathers and sisters are not all like that. "Some of them are good."

Hasan smirks. "I have yet to meet one."

"The city is full of them."

"And we will deal with those people too, in time."

"What does that mean?" she asks.

"Ask your friend Nermin Filipović that, someday," he says. "There are two sides to this war, Arrow. Ours and theirs. There is no in-between."

He returns to the window, focuses his binoculars on the street. "He's still there. Fifteen meters further south. Take your shot."

She folds her hands around her rifle, puts her eye to the scope. She finds the man, where Hasan said he would be, and aims. She now knows what she did to begin this course of events. She can pinpoint the moment at which her options began to vanish. The men on the hills told her that she hated them, and they did everything they could to make it true. She did not fight very hard. It was an easy thing to do. She wonders whether it would have been possible to behave any differently. She hopes it would have been. She hopes that, somewhere in the city, there are people who are resisting the temptation to turn these men into devils, to say that all men are like them, to oppose their very existence the way they always said the people of Sarajevo did.

But it's too late for her. There's no way to go back in time, no way to undo what has been done. Her finger rests on the trigger, and she exhales, trying to slow her racing pulse. She looks through the scope, makes a final adjustment in her aim. She sees the sniper they sent to kill the cellist, his eyes closed, his hand at his side. She hears music, and, this time, she does not fire.

"No," she says. "I won't."

She wonders if Hasan will shoot the man himself, or if he will shoot her, but he makes no move. He turns from the window, watches her pull her rifle away from the hole in the wall and begin to crawl out of the room.

"I hope you realize what you're doing," he says.

Arrow continues crawling. "I know exactly what I'm doing," she says as she reaches the inner hallway and gets to her feet. She walks to the stairway quickly, but doesn't run. She doesn't put her rifle over her shoulder, isn't sure she won't need it. The stairway is dark, and she's forced to make her way to the ground blind. Every sound she hears brings the expectation that Hasan will follow her, but he doesn't. She emerges from the stairway and walks across the lobby toward the rear entrance to the building. The two guards are still there, but again they pay her no notice. Just before she steps through the double doors and into the street, she checks her watch and sees it is almost four o'clock. Her feet hit the pavement and she begins to run.

dragan

A man is going to try to cross. He's been warned, can surely see the body of the hatless man as well as anyone, but he doesn't seem to care. He's young, perhaps a bit foolish. Dragan wonders if he gets some sort of thrill out of challenging an intersection that's known to have a sniper. It's a new sport, perhaps. The hundred-meter dash, with bullets.

Dragan sees a camera is being set up across the street. A man in a bulletproof vest stands behind the barricade and surveys the scene, calculating distances and angles, judging the visual quality of the destruction. He's clean-shaven and his clothes are immaculate. Dragan can see the neatly ironed creases in his pants from across the street. Or he thinks he can. Still, he's surprised, not at the cameraman's presence but at his location. The camera should, he thinks, be on his side of the road, the side closest to the hotel the foreign journalists stay at. The one that still has food and hot water and, often, electricity. This man has gone the long way around. It's an odd choice, and Dragan doesn't know what to make of it.

The man about to cross has seen the camera too and pauses, as though weighing whether he should wait so that his sprint can be captured on camera. He even looks down, checking his clothes. He seems to decide that his outfit isn't something he wants to wear on television, however, because he jerks forward and enters the intersection.

Everyone, including the cameraman, stops what they're doing and watches. It's not much of an audience, no more than a half-dozen people, and they've all seen this show before, with both endings. The man runs in a straight line. He's fast. A new world record? Maybe. Perhaps they will have to notify the people at Guinness.

The sniper doesn't fire, for reasons all his own, and, when the man reaches the other side, Dragan thinks the cameraman looks disappointed, because the sprinter lived and because he didn't get a shot of his run. The disappointment irritates Dragan, makes him feel like a zoo animal.

A dog comes up behind the cameraman, startling him, and Dragan smiles. The dog is uninterested, though, and continues into the street. As it nears, Dragan wonders if it's the same dog he saw earlier, with Emina. This dog has the same sense of purpose, and also appears as though it has somewhere to go. But he can't remember exactly what the first dog looked like. It could be the same. They all look the same to him now.

The dog trots across the lanes of pavement toward Dragan. As he gets close to the body of the hatless man, Dragan wonders if the dog will try to eat the corpse. It must be hungry, he thinks. Everything that is neither politician nor gangster in this city is hungry. But the dog walks past the body without even stopping to sniff at it. It's as though it wasn't even there.

Dragan hears the clink of tags as the dog passes him, sees it's wearing a collar, but it's obvious from the condition of its fur that the dog lives on the streets. It doesn't look up at Dragan or anyone else it passes, and he wonders if the dog has written mankind off altogether. Dragan wants to call out to the dog, give it something to eat, pet its fur, do something that will restore its faith in him. But he doesn't have any food, and he knows the dog won't come even if he calls it. As it turns the corner and disappears he feels a little like the way he felt when he stood watching his wife and son's bus pull into the street and fade out of sight.

He knows that he has been that dog. Ever since the war started he has walked through the streets and tried to pay as little attention as possible to his surroundings. He saw nothing he didn't have to see and did nothing he didn't have to do.

The cameraman is having a problem with his equipment. He's set his camera down on the ground, and is rummaging through a large backpack. Dragan is relieved, but then the cameraman appears to find what he was looking for and moves back to the camera. Dragan knows that the camera will be filming soon, and he knows that he doesn't want the body of the hatless man to be captured on film.

It's not that he doesn't want the world to know what's happening here. He does, or at least he agrees with the argument that the world is more likely to intervene if it is forced to see the suffering of innocents. It's just that the scene the cameraman will capture is in no way representative of what's happened here today. It's the aftermath.

A dead body won't bother anyone. It will be a curiosity, but unless some viewer knew the hatless man it will mean nothing. There's nothing in a dead body that suggests what it was like to be alive. No one will know if the man had unusually large feet, which his friends used to tease him about when he was a child. No one will know about the scar on his back he got from falling out of a tree, or that his favorite food was chocolate cake. They will not know that when he was eighteen he went on a trip with his friends from school, hitchhiked all the way to Spain, where he slept with a blond girl whose last name he never even knew, and that he would think about this often over the next thirty years, always at the strangest times, while peeling an orange or sharpening the blade of a knife or walking up a hill in the rain.

Then there are the things one doesn't mention about the dead. It will not be said that he had a quick temper, or that he sometimes cheated at his monthly card game. He was cheap. When drunk, he was cruel.

None of this will ever be said again, has simply vanished from existence. But these are the things that make a death something to be mourned. It's not just a disappearance of flesh. This, in and of itself, is easily shrugged off. When the body of the hatless man is shown on the evening news to people all over the world, they will do exactly that. They may remark on the horror, but they will, most likely, think nothing of it at all, like a dog with somewhere else to be.

Dragan looks at the body of the hatless man. He doesn't know his name, can't picture his face. He doesn't know anything about him at all. It's all conjecture. But it doesn't matter. This man is him. Or he could be. He lived in this city under siege, and he was shot crossing the street. They both did nothing when Emina needed help.

He won't allow this man's body to be filmed. He remembers what he told Emina about the cellist, why he thinks he plays. To stop something from happening. To prevent a worsening. To do what he can.

As he looks at the cameraman, however, Dragan realizes that he's missed the point. It doesn't matter what the world thinks of his city. All that matters is what he thinks. In the Sarajevo of his memory, it was completely unacceptable to have a dead man lying in the street. In the Sarajevo of today it's normal. He has been living in neither, has tried to live in a city that no longer exists, refusing to participate in the one that does.

The sniper is still there. He can't say how he knows this, but he does. Somewhere on the hills or the buildings of Grbavica he's waiting, biding his time. A man just crossed without him shooting. It means nothing. It's all a calculation. The longer he waits before shooting, the more people will venture back into the intersection. Dragan thinks it might be possible to draw a chart to express the best correlation between the number of potential targets and the time between shots. He wonders if the sniper has such a chart, perhaps on a small laminated card, tucked into the breast pocket of his jacket, or if it's just something he knows by heart.

The hatless man is close, maybe fifteen meters from him. It should be a simple thing to run to him, grab his hands, and drag him off the street. Twenty steps each way. Half a minute is all it should take. Possibly less.

He takes a deep breath and exhales. Then his feet are moving, and he's back in the street. Once again time slows down, and each time his foot surges forward it seems like an eternity passes. He can hear his feet hitting the ground. The sound slaps and echoes loud in his ears. His mouth feels dry. When he's three-quarters of the way to the body he remembers to keep his head low, and his shoulders ache as he ducks down, still running.

Dragan reaches the body of the hatless man. The soles of his shoes stick and slip in his blood. He reaches down and grabs one of his hands, lifeless and still warm. The other one is difficult to get a grip on. He loses his balance and falls. Dragan's nose is a centimeter from what remains of the head of the hatless man. A flap of skin hangs over the maw of his emptied skull like a bad toupee. For some reason, it doesn't bother Dragan. He thinks it should, knows that normally such gore would horrify him. But it isn't important. All that matters is getting the body off the street.

Something slams into the body in front of him with a flat thump. A rifle cracks. The sniper has fired, missed him by less than half a meter. Dragan grabs the hatless man's other hand and tries to get to his feet. He can't. The body is too heavy. He's able to crouch and, in an awkward sort of crab-walk, pull the body backward toward the boxcar.

He knows the sniper will fire again, but he isn't afraid. At this moment fear doesn't exist. There's no such thing as bravery. There are no heroes, no villains, no cowards. There's what he can do, and what he can't. There's right and wrong and nothing else. The world is binary. Shading will come later.

He doesn't hear the bullet hit, but he does hear the gunshot. He doesn't think he's hurt but he isn't certain. As he pulls the body of the hatless man the final few steps to safety he waits to feel some sort of pain, waits to feel the wetness of bleeding. It doesn't come. He sits down on the ground, breathing hard, sweating. He looks across the street and sees the cameraman staring at him, his mouth open. His camera is in his hands, but not on his shoulder. It hasn't captured him, or the body of the hatless man.

Good, he thinks. I will not live in a city where dead bodies lie abandoned in the streets, and you will not tell the world I do.

One of the two people on his side of the street moves toward him. The whistle of descending shells makes the person change his mind. The shells fall on the other side of the boxcar, in what's left of the abandoned army barracks. Dragan lies on his stomach, his hands over his head and his face pressed to the ground. He tries not to think about what will happen if a shell falls on his side of the barricade. The men on the hills are angry. Be angry with yourselves, Dragan thinks. You had your chance to kill me, and you'll have another chance soon.

The defenders answer back with automatic gunfire, followed by several single shots, the calling cards of countersnipers. These shots elicit more mortar fire from the men on the hills, and for a few minutes each side trades volleys until finally it's quiet, or at least relatively quiet.

Dragan sits up, brushes the dirt from his face. He wonders if this war will ever end. He wonders what it will be like if it does. Will people forget? Should they? He doesn't have any answers to these questions. But he's happy to be thinking about them. When he gets to the bakery he will ask his coworkers what they think. They may be surprised. He hasn't spoken to any of them in a long time.

He stands up, his knees and back stiff. He walks away from the body of the hatless man and picks up Emina's coat. Beside it lies the man's hat, which he picks up as well. He looks at each of them for a while. If he were to guess from the condition of the clothing, he'd think that it was Emina who was killed and the hatless man who lived. But things aren't always the way they look. Especially here. If this city is to die, it won't be because of the men on the hills, it will be because of the people in the valley. When they're content to live with death, to become what the men on the hills want them to be, then Sarajevo will die. Dragan takes Emina's coat, covers the man at his feet, and gives him back his hat.

four

kenan

Another day has just begun. Light strains its way into the apartment, where it finds Kenan in his kitchen, his hand reaching for the plastic jug containing his family's final quarter-liter of water. It's been four days since he last went to the brewery for water. It's almost always four days between trips, five if it rains. Today's trip will be different, he knows. Today is the day the cellist will play for the twenty-second and final time.

The air is cold this morning. Kenan wonders if the weather is changing. He hopes they'll have enough warm clothes to last the coming winter. Firewood will be a problem as well. He doesn't know where it will come from or how he'll get any. He'll find a way, somehow.

Kenan pushes his chair back from the kitchen table and picks up an empty water bottle. He goes over every part of it, checking for cracks or holes. He repeats the process with each of his six bottles. On the fourth he finds a small crack, which worries him. It hasn't gone all the way through, but it will, and there's no way to tell when. He decides to switch it with one of his spares. Better not to risk it.

He hears a stirring in the sitting room, where Amila and their children sleep. He hopes he hasn't woken them. It's still early. There's no reason for them to get up yet. Better they remain asleep. Who knows whether they might have to spend tonight in the shelter, where it's almost impossible to get any rest.

As quietly as he can, he picks up the last of their water and makes his way to the bathroom. He turns on the switch for the light out of habit, but nothing happens. He lights a stub of candle beside the mirror and begins to shave. Someday, he thinks, he will shave again with hot water and a sharp razor. Every day will be full of small luxuries like this, and he will enjoy every single one of them. Until then, though, he's used to shaving in the dark with cold water. It hardly bothers him anymore.

He rinses his face with the last of the water and leans in to blow out the candle. As he inhales there's a familiar tinkling sound and the lightbulb in the ceiling pops to life. A harsh yellow light fills the room, and his eyes adjust to its brightness. Kenan smiles.

He blows out the candle and goes to the closet, where a small charger is connected to a car battery. If the power stays on all day he will be able to listen to the radio for the next two weeks. If it stays on overnight they can perhaps run a light for a few hours each night. He checks the charger, watches its green light glow. The battery is charging.

Amila emerges from her bed. He smiles at her and points to the light in the ceiling. She grins, raises her hands in celebration. If the children weren't asleep, Kenan would put a CD on, something fast and cheerful, and they would shout and dance. Even though he doesn't, knowing he can is enough.

"Do you think it will stay on for long?" she asks him as he gets up and goes back into the kitchen.

He nods. "Could be. I guess there's no way to tell."

Kenan begins to tie up his bottles, three to a side.

"Be careful," she says, and he smiles.

"Of course. I always am."

The light flickers but doesn't go out. Amila rolls her eyes. "Pick up one of the large boxes of chocolates while you're out," she says, "and two dozen eggs."

"Yes, certainly. That's a lot of eggs."

"I'm going to bake a cake. A very large cake."

"Ah. In that case I'll buy some brandy as well." He leans in and kisses her.

"Good idea. Nothing goes with cake like a good brandy." She rests her hands in the small of his back, puts her head on his shoulder. "I'm tired," she says, almost whispering.

"I know," he says. "I'm tired too."

They stand like this until Kenan begins to feel time weighing down on him, and he steps back, kisses her again, and moves toward the door.

Once he's in the hall, he sits down on the steps and presses his forehead to his knees. He doesn't want to go out. He doesn't want to have to walk through the streets of his city and look at the buildings and with every step be afraid that he's about to be killed. But he has no choice. He knows that if he wants to be one of the people who rebuild the city, one of the people who have the right even to speak about how Sarajevo should repair itself, then he has to go outside and face the men on the hills. His family needs water, and he will get it for them. The city is full of people doing the same as he is, and they all find a way to continue with life. They're not cowards, and they're not heroes.

He has been to hear the cellist play every day since the shelling at the brewery. Each day at four o'clock he stands in the street with his back pressed against a wall and watches as the city is reassembled and its people awaken from hibernation. Today is the last day the cellist will play. Everyone who died in the street while waiting for bread will be accounted for. Kenan knows no one will play for the people who died at the brewery, or those who were shot crossing the street, or any of the other victims of countless attacks. It would take an army of cellists. But he's heard what there was to hear. It was enough.

Kenan stands up and makes his way down the flight of stairs. On the ground floor he stops in front of Mrs. Ristovski's door. He listens for sounds of life, wonders if she's awake, if she knows the electricity has come back on. She's usually the first to know such things.

He straightens himself, clears his throat, and knocks on the door. He hears a shuffling inside, but the door doesn't open. He knocks again, louder this time, and waits for Mrs. Ristovski to answer the door, to bring him her bottles so he can begin his long walk down the hill, through town, up the hill to the brewery and back again.

dragan

There is no way to tell which version of a lie is the truth. Is the real Sarajevo the one where people were happy, treated each other well, lived without conflict? Or is the real Sarajevo the one he sees today, where people are trying to kill each other, where bullets and bombs fly down from the hills and the buildings crumble to the ground? Dragan can only ask the question. He doesn't think there's any way to know for sure.

It's past noon. He's been at this intersection for over two hours now. It seems like days. Stuck in a sort of no-man's-land, kept but not kept from going to the bakery, where a small loaf of bread waits for him. He can cross whenever he likes. At no time has anyone come and said, No, Dragan, you can't cross. It's always been his decision.

He knows which lie he will tell himself. The city he lives in is full of people who will someday go back to treating each other like humans. The war will end, and when it's looked back upon it will be with regret, not with fond memories of faded glory. In the meantime, he will continue to walk the streets.

Streets that will not have dead and discarded bodies lying in them. He will behave now as he hopes everyone will someday behave. Because civilization isn't a thing that you build and then there it is, you have it forever. It needs to be built constantly, re-created daily. It vanishes far more quickly than he ever would have thought possible. And if he wishes to live, he must do what he can to prevent the world he wants to live in from fading away. As long as there's war, life is a preventative measure.

The cameraman has left, gone to a busier intersection. He needs people to take a chance and get shot, or, shot at, or even, if that doesn't happen, at least look like they think they're going to die. Eventually the cameraman will get what he wants. It's only a matter of time.

Dragan makes up his mind. He's going across. He's not going to let the men on the hills stop him. These are his streets, and he'll walk them as he sees fit. In little less than four hours the cellist will play for the final time.

He adjusts his coat and shakes one foot, which has fallen partially asleep. The sky is beginning to cloud over, and there's a slight chill in the air. He steps into the intersection. His shoes scuff on the pavement, and somewhere close by a car accelerates to a high pitch. A small bird flies overhead. Dragan is not running. He knows he should be, is aware that the sniper is likely still in his perch. He could be in his sights right now. All it would take is a squeeze of a trigger and he'd be dead.

His feet don't respond to his mind's urgings. He can't run. At a leisurely pace his body carries him across the road, past where Emina was shot, toward the other side. He could be walking down any street in the world. To a casual observer he's just an old man out for a stroll.

This is anything but the case. Dragan is terrified, has never been so afraid. But he can't force himself to move any faster. After a while he stops trying. He keeps his eyes on the safe area he's heading toward, and he tries not to think about anything other than putting one foot in front of the other.

He begins to understand why he isn't running. If he doesn't run, then he's alive again. The Sarajevo he wants to live in is alive again. If he runs, then it won't matter how many bodies lie in the streets. Perhaps the people watching him will think he's snapped, that he's gone catatonic and doesn't care anymore whether he lives or dies. They'd be wrong. He cares now more than ever.

He's been asleep since the war began. He knows this now. In defending himself from death he lost his grip on life. He thinks of Emina, risking her life to deliver expired pills to someone she's never met. Of the young man who ran into the street to save her when she was shot. Of the cellist who plays for those killed in a mortar attack. He could run now, but he doesn't.

He waits for gunfire, for the bullet that will hit him. But it never comes. He's both surprised and not surprised. There's just never any way to tell. It doesn't matter. If it comes, it will come. If it doesn't, he will be one of the lucky ones.

Dragan reaches the opposite side of the road. It hasn't taken him long at all, but it seems a good portion of his life has gone by. It's a good thing the cameraman has gone. He knows he's created horrible television. An old man walking across a street, with nothing happening. Hardly news.

He walks west, toward the bakery. He should be there in ten more minutes. But then his hand feels a small plastic pill bottle and a scrap of paper with an address in his pocket, and he knows he'll be a little late. Still, no more than a half hour. He'll get his bread, and then he'll come back this way, whether the sniper's working or not. On his way home he'll make a small detour to the street just south of the market and wait for four o'clock, so he can tell Emina what happened on the last day the cellist played.

Dragan smiles as he passes by an elderly man. The man doesn't meet his gaze, keeps his eyes on the ground.

"Good afternoon," Dragan says, his voice bright.

The man looks up. He seems surprised.

"Good afternoon," Dragan repeats.

The man nods, smiles, and wishes him the same.

arrow

Arrow blinks. She has been waiting for a long time. She slept well, didn't wake even once during the night. There's one sound she's been listening for, and it's here. Footsteps echo in the hall outside her door, heavy boots coming up the stairs. They're making an effort to be quiet, but the stairwell isn't helping, its acoustics unaccommodating to the aims of men requiring stealth. Arrow opens her eyes. It's still early in the morning, not quite seven o'clock.

It's been ten days since she walked away from Hasan on the fourteenth floor of the Parliament Building, ten days since she deserted Edin Karaman's unit of murderers. This is the first night she's slept in her apartment since then, and already they've found her. She's a little surprised. She didn't imagine they'd be so efficient.

Her father's gun is on the bedside table beside her. It's loaded and ready, but her hand stays at her side, under her pile of blankets. She wonders what the weather will be like today.

Yesterday it seemed it might rain, but there's never any way to tell what will happen the next day until it comes. She hopes it rains. The city could use the water.

They've been hunting her for ten days now, and they have found her because she has allowed them to. They knew where she was all along, knew she was in one of the buildings above the cellist, but they couldn't find her, no matter how many times they looked. Twice she had Edin Karaman's head in her sights, but she never pulled the trigger. She hasn't fired her rifle since killing the sniper the men on the hills sent for the cellist. But she would have, if necessary, and she believes her presence kept him alive.

He played for twenty-two days, just as he said he would. Every day at four o'clock in the afternoon, regardless of how much fighting was going on around him. Some days he had an audience. Other days there was so much shelling that no one in their right mind would linger in the street. It didn't appear to make any difference to him. He always played exactly the same way.

The only variation in his routine was on the last day. She lay concealed in her hiding spot, invisible. She felt him enter the street, but before he began to play she knew no one was going to shoot him. The men on the hills had given up. Her hands relaxed and her finger fell from the trigger. As the cellist began to play she looked down at the street. It was full of people.

No one moved. They all stood motionless, and though it was clear to her that they were listening intently, it also seemed as though they weren't entirely there.

Arrow let the slow pulse of the vibrating strings flood into her. She felt the lament raise a lump in her throat, fought back tears. She inhaled sharp and fast. Her eyes watered, and the notes ascended the scale. The men on the hills, the men in the city, herself, none of them had the right to do the things they'd done. It had never happened. It could not have happened. But she knew these notes. They had become a part of her. They told her that everything had happened exactly as she knew it had, and that nothing could be done about it. No grief or rage or noble act could undo it. But it could all have been stopped. It was possible. The men on the hills didn't have to be murderers. The men in the city didn't have to lower themselves to fight their attackers. She didn't have to be filled with hatred. The music demanded that she remember this, that she know to a certainty that the world still held the capacity for goodness. The notes were proof of that.

Arrow closed her eyes, and when she opened them the music was over. In the street, the cellist sat on his stool for a very long time. He was crying. His head leaned forward and a few strands of inky hair fell across his brow. One hand moved to cover his face while the other cradled the body of the cello. After a while he stood up, and he walked over to the pile of flowers that had been steadily growing since the day the mortar fell. He looked at it for a while, and then dropped his bow into the pile. No one on the street moved. They held their breath, waiting for him to say something. But the cellist didn't speak. There was nothing left for him to say. He turned, picked up his stool, and went through the door to his apartment without looking back at the street. Slowly people began to move, and one by one they left the street to return to their lives.

The footsteps are at the top of the stairs now, just outside her door. Arrow looks again at the gun on her night table. If she were to use it, she knows exactly what would happen. The men on the other side of the door would die. Every one of them would die and she'd step over their bodies and out into the street. It would take only a few seconds. It would be the easiest thing in the world.

But she isn't going to pick up the gun. It sits on the night table partly out of habit, and partly because she wants them to know that she was armed and could have fought back. She's not sure they'll notice this clue. It doesn't matter. It matters only that she leaves it.

She wonders what her life might have been like if there had been no war, if the men on the hills hadn't decided that they needed to be reviled, or that the answer to their aspirations of victimhood lay in guns and tanks and grenades. Maybe she'd have gotten married. Maybe she'd have gone on to graduate school, had a good job, lived in a nice apartment, and gone to the theater in the evenings with her friends. There could have been children. She likes children, or she used to. The possibilities were endless.

The possibilities now, however, are at an end. If she picks up the gun and kills the men on the other side of the door, she will become a fugitive. And sooner or later, she will either have to kill again or she will be caught. In the meantime, necessity will force her to hate her pursuers. And Arrow will not let that happen. Whether they are on the hills or in the city, no one will tell her who to hate.

After the cellist disappeared, Arrow went down to the street, not caring whether anyone saw her. She looked at the cobblestones, the shattered windows, the pile of flowers. She didn't think of anything, couldn't think of anything she hadn't already gone over a thousand times. So she just stood there. The cellist wouldn't be back tomorrow. There would be no more concerts in the street. She was disappointed it was over. Arrow leaned down and placed her rifle beside the cellist's bow.

In a few seconds the door will open. At least four men, maybe more, will burst through and, as quickly as they can, they will fire as many bullets into her as possible. It won't take long, only a few seconds, and afterward they will feel sheepish at how nervous they were about the whole thing.

She hears one of them take a step back, knows he's about

to kick in the door. She closes her eyes, recalls the notes she heard only yesterday, a melody that is no longer there but feels very close. Her lips move, and a moment before the door splinters off its hinges she says, her voice strong and quiet, "My name is Alisa."

afterword

It is important to note that this novel is not a historically accurate timeline of the Siege of Sarajevo. It is impossible for the events that take place in this book to have occurred in the order they do. For necessity's sake I have compressed three years into under a month. I hope, however, that the spirit of the book is true.

At four o'clock in the afternoon on May 27, 1992, during the Siege of Sarajevo, several mortar shells struck a group of people waiting to buy bread behind the market on Vase Miskina. Twenty-two people were killed and at least seventy were wounded. For the next twenty-two days Vedran Smailović, a renowned local cellist, played Albinoni's Adagio in G Minor at the site in honor of the dead. His actions inspired this novel, but I have not based the character of the cellist on the real Smailović, who was able to leave Sarajevo in December of 1993 and now lives in Northern Ireland.

The name Arrow comes from a Radio Denmark documentary entitled *Sniper*. A female sniper named Arrow (Strijela) was interviewed for the program, though very little information was given about her. I tried to locate her but failed. She may be dead. In any case the character of Arrow in this novel is my own invention.

The Siege of Sarajevo, the longest city siege in the history of modern warfare, stretched from April 5, 1992, to February 29, 1996. The United Nations estimates that approximately 10,000 people were killed and 56,000 wounded. An average of 329 shells hit the city each day, with a one-day high of 3,777 on July 22, 1993. In a city of roughly half a million people, 10,000 apartments were destroyed, and 100,000 were damaged. Twenty-three percent of all buildings were seriously damaged, and a further 64 percent partially. As of October 2007 the leaders of the Bosnian Serb Army, Radovan Karadžić and Ratko Mladić, are still at large, despite having been charged in 1996 with war crimes, genocide, and crimes against humanity by the International Criminal Tribunal for the former Yugoslovia in The Hague.

I owe a deep debt of gratitude to Dinko Mesković, Sana Mesković, Miroslav Nenadić, and Olga Nesić-Nenadić in Vancouver, and Alija Ramović in Sarajevo for the countless hours they spent telling me stories, showing me places, and trying to teach me to think like a Sarajevan. There is much of them in this book, but any errors in fact or fiction are mine alone. Many thanks to Sanja Ramović for loaning me her father.

I would like to thank Henry Dunow for his zealous representation and overall excellentness. I believe Michael Heyward to be the greatest Australian ever to live. Thanks to Mandy Brett, Sarah McGrath, Ravi Mirchandani, and Rosemary Shipton for their editorial advice and enthusiasm. To Diane Martin, my friend and editor, I owe a debt I will never be able to repay, but I will continue to try.

Anne Beilby, Nina Ber-Donkor, Sarah Castleton, Marita Dachsel, Louise Dennys, Lara Galloway, Angelika Glover, Anthony Goff, Nancy Lee, Jeff Moores, Emiko Morita, Adrienne Phillips, Sarah Stein, Timothy Taylor, John Vigna, Patricia Young, Terence Young, and Hal Wake each have helped me make this book better. Friends and family have met my absence, irritation, and distractedness with kindness and encouragement. The University of British Columbia Creative Writing Program, and my colleagues there, are irreplaceable. The Simon Fraser University Writer's Studio, University of Victoria Department of Writing, and the Sage Hill Writing Experience have employed and enriched me. Thank you. I gratefully acknowledge the financial assistance of the Canada Council for the Arts.

—S.G.